"*Thistledom* is a great story! I enjoyed all the characters as if they were personal friends."

- Megan, Royal Oak, Michigan

"The characters and scenes in *Thistledom* are so real, it's like reading a movie."

- Irene, Hershey, Pennsylvania

"The descriptions within *Thistledom* are so vivid, they truly fire one's imagination to the point of belief."

- Teresa, Chicago, Illinois

"My journey through Thistledom with such lovable, unforgettable characters was truly enchanting – an inspiring tale for all ages. A must read!"

- Francis, The Land of the Mitten

"Loved reading *Thistledom: A Kingdom Is Born*; felt sad when the story ended because I hated to leave this place. Now I've learned that *Thistledom* is a series. I can't wait to return to the Land of the Nobbies!"

- Debbie, Palm Harbor, Florida

Saint Paul's Press, LLC
Livonia, Michigan

# VOLUME I

# "A Kingdom is Born"

### John LaCroix

Saint Paul's Press, LLC
P.O. Box 530547 Livonia, MI 48153

www.saintpaulspress.com

*Thistledom, Volume*
Copyright © 2007 by John W. LaCroix. All rights reserved.

No part of this publication may be reproduced, stored in a retrieval system or transmitted in any way by any means, electronic, mechanical, photocopy, recording or otherwise without the prior permission of the author except as provided by USA copyright law.

This novel is a work of fiction. Names, descriptions, entities and incidents included in the story are products of the author's imagination. Any resemblance to actual persons, events and entities is entirely coincidental.

Word definitions taken from the *Encyclopedia Britannica Ultimate Reference Suite*, 2004 DVD: *Merriam-Webster's Collegiate Dictionary*, Tenth Edition. *Webster's Seventh New Collegiate Dictionary*, G. & C. Merriam Company, Publishers, Springfield, MA., U.S.A. 1965.

First edition ISBN: 978-1-60462-563-3

Published by St. Paul's Press, LLC
P.O. Box 530547
Livonia, MI 48153

Book design copyright © 2009 St. Paul's Press, LLC All Rights Reserved.

Printed by PAGE LITHO, 6445 East Vernor, Detroit, Michigan 48207

Published in the United States of America

Library of Congress Number: 2010912806

Second Edition
ISBN: 978-0-9740355-7-4

# Dedication

To Natalie through whom all good things have come for forty years; to John and Sara, James and Deana, and Margaret and Daniel for your continual unfailing love and respect, and for the wondrous "seeds of promise" you have given to our family; and finally to Lee Ann who has steadfastly supported me and my causes without reservation in every phase of this life.

# Dedication

*Thistledom*'s inspiration flows from the lifelong friendship of Rev. Paul F. Chateau, his extended family, and a labor of love called "Le Grande Chateau Castle." Thank you for your endless faith and support from our youth, your strong voice, and unwavering brotherly concern. You are a priceless gift for which I and my family are eternally grateful. Thank God that the friendships forged in faith and nurtured by love endure for eternity. Special thanks to Nicholas Sharkey and Margaret Mikula for their critiques and ideas; to John LaCroix, Jr., for his creative contributions; and to Natalie for her understanding and great patience all those afternoons and evenings I had to travel to Thistledom.

# Table of Contents

Foreword . . . . . . . . . . . . . . . . . . . . . . . . . . . . 1
Preface . . . . . . . . . . . . . . . . . . . . . . . . . . . . . 3

A Seed's Power Lies in Its Promise . . . . . . . . . 5
Marks of the Nobby Master . . . . . . . . . . . . . 22
Sons of the Promise . . . . . . . . . . . . . . . . . . . 28
The Seed Is Lost . . . . . . . . . . . . . . . . . . . . . 37
Binder's Trail . . . . . . . . . . . . . . . . . . . . . . . 46
No One Stands at the End of the Rainbow . . 66
A Kingdom Is Born . . . . . . . . . . . . . . . . . . . 81
The Mystery of the Bog . . . . . . . . . . . . . . . . 96
DuBois Castle—The Vision . . . . . . . . . . . . 124
DuBois Castle—Fruition . . . . . . . . . . . . . . 148
DuBois Castle—Homecoming . . . . . . . . . . 167
Pillars Fall in Thistledom . . . . . . . . . . . . . . 177

Epilogue: "Seeds of Promise Must
    Bloom in Adversity" . . . . . . . . . . . . . . . . 216

Glossary: Words, Terms, Tables,
    and Charts . . . . . . . . . . . . . . . . . . . . . . . 218
Table of Nobby Measurement . . . . . . . . . . . 247
Nobby Geographical Locations
    in Thistledom . . . . . . . . . . . . . . . . . . . . . 249
Map of the Kingdom . . . . . . . . . . . . . . . . . 251

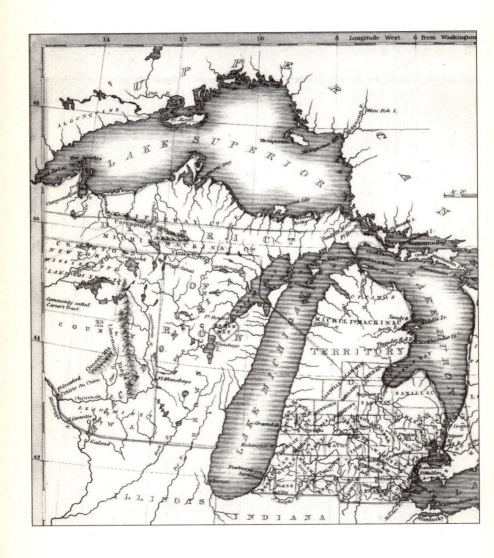

# Foreword

Sit back in your favorite easy chair. Put another log on the fire. Relax for a few hours and let John LaCroix's new book *Thistledom* transport you to the Land of the Mitten—a book that teaches many important lessons for those living in the troubled twenty-first century.

Free your imagination as you read about the Nobbies, Troggs and Doogles, royalty, and everyday heroes and evil villains who all reside in the Kingdom of Thistledom. This book is part fast-moving adventure, part generational history, part suspense thriller, and always inspirational as the reader follows the chronicles of five generations of the Royal Family DuBois.

The story is told in an easy-to-follow flashback style as the elderly sage Lord Norbert tells Princess Julia about the history of her family on the night before she turns sixteen. Julia knows little about her ancestors and even less about her own father and why she had been chosen as queen ten years earlier. By the end of the book, Julia—along with the reader—will be enthralled by a story

John LaCroix

that quickly moves between great victories and devastating setbacks for the DuBois Family. In the end we learn the meaning of a special message inscribed on a pendant and the importance of the beam of the North Star.

Perhaps the most fascinating part of the book describes in intricate detail the building of the DuBois Castle with its rockwood beams, central courtyard, high towers, large moat, secret tunnels, Grand Gathering Hall and hidden staircases.

Author John LaCroix draws on his many skills and rich background as a son, brother, husband, father, grandfather, author, artist, musician, craftsman, and religious education leader in weaving a fascinating tale. Anyone with a little religious training will recognize the themes of devastation, sacrifice, and redemption and the importance of living your life according to a plan written by a Higher Power.

Let's not wait any longer! It's time to turn the page and experience the wonderful lives of those fortunate to live in Thistledom.

                Nick Sharkey
                Retired Director of Global Corporate News for Ford Motor Company
                Former Executive Editor of the *Observer* and *Eccentric* newspapers in Michigan

# Preface

There is no greater place than the Realm of Imagination. To travel here is to be godlike. To breathe its air fuels that marvelous fire called life burning deep within each of us.

It is a wondrous place without borders, which can be magical and mysterious, funny and frightening, and full of adventure and suspense—all at the same time. It can be the domain of beauty and charm, or a place of pain and unspeakable horror. While a visitor in this Land, we can, and often do, experience the full gamut of human emotions.

The power of this invisible force is its amazing ability to mix and mingle fantasy and fact, creating a new and exciting world of make-believe reality. While this world within is not real, what we feel *is* real. We can learn much about ourselves, and whatever we do learn, we can bring back home with us: things like greater understanding, how it would actually feel to trade places with others, to share adventure and experiences, or even to get a glimpse of our own capacity for love and hate.

Imagination, however, is a strange gift. It can wither and die when not used. It is not a treasure to be safeguarded or stored away in a dark, secret place. Imagination is a treasure that thrives only with use, and ironically, it grows even greater when shared and given away. It is truly a gift for the young of heart of every age.

The Kingdom of Thistledom is a land where life is loved, as well as lived; where the spirit within is the real measure of one's greatness. It is a land where "seeds of promise" are sprinkled for all those who would seek them. They are there to find, harvest, nurture, and replant. Above all, it is a place not unlike our own. It is a land of opportunity, challenges, and choices. Welcome to the marvelous Kingdom of Thistledom!

# A Seed's Power Lies in Its Promise

Lord Norbert, a very old sage, and Nobby Queen Julia of Thistledom are alone in a private sitting room in DuBois Castle. It is nearing dusk on the fifth day of *Colors*, the eve of Queen Julia's sixteenth birthday. There is much on her mind.

"Lord Norbert, tomorrow I'll be sixteen. I'm so excited, I can hardly believe it!"

"I know! Time passes so quickly, Julia, but remember that it has two faces. It seems to take forever when we are waiting for something. Yet, it's a mere wink of the eye when looking back at the past."

"I'm so happy, Lord Norbert, but still very much puzzled."

"About what?"

"What happened to my father? Why was I chosen as Queen of Thistledom ten cycles ago? You promised to tell me on my sixteenth birthday. I know, my birthday isn't really until tomorrow, but it will be so hectic tomorrow, we won't even have time to talk. Isn't tonight close enough?"

"Yes, I suppose it is, but the embers in the fireplace are dying. You are right about tomorrow. It surely will be hectic! Is now really a good time?"

"Lord Norbert, I've been waiting for this moment *forever*!"

"There is so much to tell you; so many things you need to know. I hardly know where to begin!"

"Can you begin with my father? How and when did he die? I know he, King Paul, and many other ancestors are buried in the crypt below the castle, but little is really known about their lives and deeds."

"Without some background, you wouldn't understand his life nor death nor his place in Nobby history. There is so much to remember…so many stories to tell…so much for you to learn. I hardly know where to begin."

Julia moved quickly to the hearth, selected several logs and gingerly stacked them in the smoldering embers, carefully shying away from sparks as they danced frantically up the chimney toward the cold black night. She stretched for two shorter logs to place crisscross atop the others. Lord Norbert settled back in his chair. Grabbing a small rug, Julia scrunched it into a soft pile and slid right up close to his feet. The new fire would feel good, but love has a special warmth.

"I'm so lucky to have you, Lord Norbert. You're so good and wise. How long have you lived in this castle? I guess as long as anyone can remember! Right?"

A wee smile parted her lips as her thoughts returned to childhood. She remembered her grandfather, King Isidore, holding her and older sister, Emily, on his lap while Lord Norbert read aloud, making stories come alive with his many voices and animal sounds. She also had dim memories of Grandfather walking along the moat with Lord Norbert in the early evening as the sun fell behind the mountain. It seemed the two walked and talked a lot. Everyone loved Lord Norbert! It was very easy to do.

Loud crackling from the fireplace ended her brief sojourn. Reflections of newborn flames flickered merrily in Lord Norbert's soft green eyes. Shadows darted and danced about the room. His face was radiant, framed by a halo of downy-white hair.

"Nobbies have been here in the Land of the Mitten for generations, living in harmony with nature and using its gifts wisely. We understand nature and work with it. We do not try to change nature. Mining and farming became our mainstays. These were our special skills because we learned to do both without scarring the land."

"Lord Norbert, have Nobbies always lived in Thistledom? If not, where did we come from? Are there any written records for us to read? Are the records hidden some place here in the castle?"

"No, Nobbies have not always lived in Thistledom because there wasn't always a Thistledom. King Theodore was our first king, the one who established Thistledom."

"Well, what happened before King Theodore? Where were Nobbies then, in another kingdom?"

Lord Norbert smiled, "No, our ancestors always lived here on this mountain and throughout several regions, but there was neither castle nor kingdom."

"So, how far back does our history go?"

"Good questions, Julia. Here's what I know. Long ago, a young Nobby named Zygmunt lived nearby in Thistleville, a tiny hamlet named after the prickly plant, which is covered with those pretty purple and yellow flowers you love so much."

"They are beautiful!"

"They are much more than just beautiful. We have learned important secrets from the simple thistle plant."

"What kind of secrets?"

"I bet you didn't know that Nobbies once used kernels of corn to measure things instead of thistle leaves. It's true! Then someone noticed that it took eight average size kernels, laid side by side, to equal the length of a single thistle leaf. We still use kernels as the measure for things smaller than a thistle leaf, but the single leaf has become our basic standard of measurement. You, for instance, are four leafs and six kernels tall. In fact, the Kingdom of Thistledom owes its very existence to these marvelous friends of nature."

"Who was this Zygmunt? Did he begin Thistledom?"

"In a way he did. Zygmunt was a giant Nobby. It took seven full thistle leaves to stretch from his head to toes. No Nobby before or since has been so tall—well, except one."

"What did Zygmunt do?"

"He was as brave as he was tall. Nobbies from other villages often would call for help when a rogue rat or renegade hawk posed a danger. He never refused."

"What would he do?"

"He'd stand alone motionless in the open, bow his head and close his eyes—an easy, irresistible target. Mere seconds seemed like hours while a rat crept closer or a hawk circled ever lower overhead. From a safe distance, villagers hid and watched without a sound as the tension mounted. At the very last instant before the strike, Zygmunt would open his eyes and stare. As his arms rose into the air, rushing rats fell at his feet, swooping hawks careened to a stop, only to encase him harmlessly in a flurry of outstretched wings. Though a few actually did touch him, none ever harmed him. After a few anxious moments staring eye to eye, he would wave his arm and the would-be attacker would race away. It was amazing! Most astonishing, they never came back!"

Julia could feel her own heart racing. "Where did he learn how to do this? How did he know when other villages needed him?"

"Zygmunt explained only that this power was a special gift given to him. As for how he knew about the dangers in other villages, you will learn for yourself tomorrow on your sixteenth birthday."

Just as in Julia's childhood, the power in Lord Norbert's voice brought scenes long past back to life. She could feel the chill in the forest air and smell the soothing scent of pine as Lord Norbert began the story of Zygmunt.

From the age of four, Zygmunt was raised by his grandfather because both parents had disappeared while

## A Seed's Power Lies in Its Promise

on a trip near the base of the mountain. The whole village searched night and day for an entire period. They were never found. All Zygmunt had to remember them by was a gold chain and pendant given him at birth by his father. It bore the image of a thistle plant and the words: *A Seed's Power Lies in Its Promise.* Chester took it from a small box and placed it around Zygmunt's neck the day after they disappeared. Zygmunt never took it off.

Chester, a widower, was a fearless woodsman, and his grandson grew up in the forest. Animals became his friends and trees were home, especially the boughs of the gentle firs. Zygmunt was nearly ten when a violent nighttime thunderstorm exploded over their heads. Lightning snapped like a whip and flashed through the trees. Dark shadowy monsters seemed to lunge at him from everywhere. Legs numb and his insides shaking with fear, Zygmunt hid under a blanket until the saving light of morning. A few days later, while watching the first glorious rays of sunlight at the majestic calm of daybreak, his grandfather whispered:

"Zygmunt, are you not afraid of the sunrise?"

"No, Grandfather! It's so quiet and beautiful."

"You should not fear storms either. *Fear is born in the mind and only ignorance gives it life.* The less you know, the more fear grows. Make no mistake! Fear can paralyze your mind and body like it did the other night. The only real cure for fear is knowledge, not running away nor hiding your head. Son, there is a big difference between a shadow and what makes it.

"In truth, you saw only shadows the other night during the storm. There were no monsters, only tree branches waving wildly in the wind. Shadows are only distorted reflections of other things. When you learn to see what makes shadows, you do not need to hide. Shadows are important because they come from light. Learning about shadows teaches us how to find truth in this world."

Zygmunt mastered this and many other lessons. Life in the woods for the next six cycles of seasons became a priceless heritage. He learned to read books as well as he read signs in nature.

One evening near the end of *Colors*, they set up camp in a small clearing ringed by majestic pines. At dusk, a lone figure appeared. He was very old, much older than Zygmunt's grandfather. It was strange because Nobbies don't usually travel alone, especially at night in the woods, even though their green eyes see as well in the dark as in daylight. Zygmunt wondered if the old Nobby was lost. The elderly stranger asked if he might share supper and the warmth of the campfire. Since the time of *Fire* was close, the night air was quite cold. Chester nodded approval and the figure approached.

"Good evening! Thank you for your kindness, Chester. And how are you this evening, Zygmunt?"

# A Seed's Power Lies in Its Promise

Zygmunt looked up, *How does this stranger know both our names? Perhaps Grandfather knew him when they were both young?*

Chester prepared their meal, smiling quietly as he heard the stranger respond directly to Zygmunt's thoughts, "No, son, I am not lost. I have been admiring your skills and knowledge for many days. You would like to know if your grandfather and I were friends in our youth?"

For the first time in recent memory, a strange tightness gripped Zygmunt's throat, the back of his neck grew warm, and a shaky feeling filled his chest. Once again, he recognized fear. He jumped to his feet, towering over the old Nobby.

"Sir, what is your name and why have you been following us? There is little that Grandfather and I do not hear or see in these woods. What do you want?"

"My name is Francis. I've been awaiting your arrival for a long time. Your grandfather brought you here to meet me."

Now, Zygmunt was really confused! His thoughts raced. "What's going on? Grandfather!"

Francis stood up. "Zygmunt, be not afraid! I am your friend. You are a special Nobby, very important to all of us. Your grandfather has worked hard these many seasons to teach you our ways and the ways of nature. Now you are ready! I asked him to bring you to me for your final preparation, and to give you a very special gift. A warning, however! You must use this gift for others, or you will lose it. Know this, too. The power I give you will become even greater in time when passed on yet to another."

Francis had first appeared as an ominous stranger in the darkness of a new moon. A second new moon had since passed and grown to full light. Time was but a wink. Nearly through the period of *Wind*, they had barely noticed the change in the season. It had been a warm, wonderful time of swapped tales, great meals, and marvelous lessons from Francis. The season and weather were unmistakably changing, however, and soon the time of *Snow* would begin with the shortest day of the entire cycle. As always, the Shortest Day would mark the beginning of the cold, dark *Shiver* quarter, and its frigid rule over both land and sky.

Perhaps the cold air caused the change in Francis. He spoke more quickly now. A serious tone in his voice betrayed an eerie urgency. As the evening fire dwindled, Zygmunt retired to the gentle arms of a familiar blue spruce. The blackness of a cloudless sky brought the stars close enough to touch—an awesome illusion. Crisp night air and the soothing scent of fir, however, were just too alluring even for this avid stargazer. Heavy eyelids closed as a warm blanket covered his head. The body was at rest, but his mind would run on through the night. Francis' deep, gentle voice could be heard again, even in his sleep:

## A Seed's Power Lies in Its Promise

"Zygmunt, I wish I could answer all your questions, but I cannot. Long ago, large tomes made from birch bark contained our entire Nobby history. They were kept high above the ground tucked safely inside the trunk of a giant oak tree. At some point, the exact time is uncertain, lightning struck, igniting a terrible forest fire. Nobbies fled safely, but without the tomes. This catastrophe was followed by a long period of heavy rains and then mud slides. By the time Nobbies could safely return, the charred library had fallen prey to rain and ravenous moths. Once packed with history and tradition, the written records were now but ashes and a few burnt fragments—the old oak had become a cavernous wooden tomb filled only with long lost secrets."

As Zygmunt dreamed, a great emptiness filled his heart. He heard himself asking, "Couldn't anybody remember what was in the tomes, at least some of the most important parts? What about the fragments?"

Francis' answer in the world of dreams remained unchanged, "There weren't many large fragments, but the largest made note of some type of giant troll called a Trogg. It said little else. There were only a few isolated words on the parchment: *roamed, terror, fou-smel*. For a time, elderly scholars were able to recall some stories, but not nearly enough before they died. Thankfully though, we do know how our Nobby calendar began.

"The Land of the Mitten has so many different kinds of weather that affect our farming and mining. Big changes in temperature occur. We came to recognize four different and distinct time-periods: *Shiver*, *Awakening*, *Suntime*, and *Color*. Taken together they form a longer time period known as the cycle. Of course, a single cycle is divided quite naturally into these four seasons, each lasting about the same amount of days.

"In the warmer seasons, the sun's path in the sky gets higher every day and is almost right overhead at midday. It reaches the highest point above the southern horizon only one time a year at the very beginning of the *Suntime* quarter on the first day of *Sun*, which is the longest day in the entire cycle. After this day, the midday sun begins to drop ever so slowly down lower in the sky each day until it reaches its lowest path across the sky on the southern horizon. This lowest path on the southern horizon always occurs on the first day of the *Shiver* quarter and is always the shortest day in the entire cycle. It is also the beginning of the *Festival of Light*. With this information scholars decided to establish a Nobby cycle having four equal quarters, each with ninety-one days, except the *Shiver* quarter, which has extra days.

"The first quarter marked by the cold was called *Shiver* and always started with the shortest day of the cycle. The *Shiver* season was further divided into three periods: time of *Snow* (thirty-two days), time of *Ice* (thirty days), and time of *Thaw* (thirty days). The predominant colors reflected in traditional Nobby dress for this season became the black of night, the white of snow, and the deep green of the firs and pines.

## A Seed's Power Lies in Its Promise

"The second quarter was called *Awakening* in honor of the new life springing from the earth. *Awakening* also was divided into three periods: time of *Buds* (thirty-one days), time of *Rain* (thirty days), and time of *Flowers* (thirty days). Traditional dress now reflected the colors of green grass, red rose, and wild violet flowers that danced in the meadows. It is a season to make new friends.

"*Suntime* is the third quarter, a favorite season of the young and begins always with the longest day. Its three periods are: time of *Sun* (thirty-one days), time of *Heat* (thirty days), and time of *Harvest* (thirty days). Nobby fashions now follow the yellow of the sun, blue sky, white clouds, and pink flowers. *Suntime* is for rest, relaxation, and study.

"The last quarter, *Color*, was named for the falling leaves and began with the time of *Colors* (thirty-one days), followed by time of *Fire* (thirty days), and finally the time of *Wind* (thirty days). This is our most colorful season filled with the purple, orange, brown, yellow and red hues of leaves before they fall to the ground forming a blanket from the *Shiver* chill. Keep this little schedule. It will help you remember many things. It is *The Nobby Cycle*."

John LaCroix

# Nobby Calendar of Seasons

Shiver Season – colors are black, white, and dark green
- Snow    (32 days) – The Shortest Day – Festival of Light
- Ice    (30 days)
- Thaw    (30 days)

Awakening Season – colors are red, violet and light green
- Buds    (30 days)
- Rain    (30 days)
- Flowers    (31 days)

Suntime Season – colors are yellow, blue, white and pink
- Sun    (30 days) – The Longest Day
- Heat    (30 days)
- Harvest    (31 days)

Color Season – colors are purple, orange, brown, yellow and red
- Colors    (30 days)
- Fire    (30 days)
- Wind    (31 days)

## A Seed's Power Lies in Its Promise

"Francis, why does the period of *Snow* that begins the *Shiver* season always have more days than the other periods of the cycle?"

"Zygmunt, our Nobby calendar celebrates many happydays throughout the cycle, but none more exciting than the *Festival of Light*, a magical time at the very beginning of *Shiver* season when the North Star shines directly above on the night of the shortest day. A light beam, very faint at first, glows from the star to a spot on the ground. Because the light always reappears a second night, scholars added one extra day to the time of *Snow* giving it a total of thirty-two days."

Zygmunt nodded. "I see, so *Snow* can have as many as thirty-two days."

"That is true, Zygmunt, but only most of the time. The *Festival of Light* always lasts for these two days and nights. But at every fourth cycle, the light strangely reappears a third night as well. Thus, a second day and night are added at this special time giving *Snow* a total of *thirty-three* days during this special cycle. The *Festival of Light* is the greatest happyday period in the Land of the Mitten, yet the marvelous light from the North Star remains a mystery. The glow of the beam grows in intensity as the sky darkens. Everyone can clearly see the beam and how brightly it lights the ground in the distance, but no one can actually find the spot and stand in the light. It's like trying to touch the end of a rainbow.

"There was so much important information in those tomes. Even so, all was not lost! Nobby culture survives even without full knowledge of our history. In fact, it has endured and prospered.

"Throughout our history, young Nobbies with extraordinary abilities have always appeared to lead us through trials and danger. Their special knowledge is shared and passed onward in an unbroken chain. Each is the lone custodian of sacred Nobby wisdom and power until it is time their gifts pass to another. The life-links in this unbroken chain, however, are of many different lengths. It is he who made the North Star, as well as the heavens, who mysteriously chooses these Nobbies and sets the time of their service."

Zygmunt found it hard to breathe. *The air is stifling, like it gets sometimes in the mines*, he thought. He remembered then what Francis had said about mining being the source of Nobby wealth, and that it also held secrets that one day would give rise to a kingdom. Nobbies mined for useful things like salt and coal, sometimes, gold, silver, and copper for decorating and cooking. There was another material, too, that looked like salt, but wasn't. The particles were much too hard and didn't have any taste. *What did Francis mean? What secrets?*

The mine was getting stuffier. The air was stale and it really was hard to breathe. Zygmunt began to flail his arms wildly, gasping for air. As the thistledown blanket fell from his head, a torrent of cold night air rushed to his lungs and he awoke. Startled, he looked up at the stars, mumbled something softly to himself, pulled the blanket tight to his ears, and fell back into a very deep and peaceful sleep.

# Marks of the Nobby Master

Only Francis knew their destination. The *Shiver* quarter was upon them and with it, the *Festival of Light*. For the past few days, Francis had been leading them in the general direction of Thistleville. They are still in the deep woods. The days are growing much shorter; nights are long and cold. There is snow in the sky.

As Zygmunt awoke, it was the first day of *Snow*, the shortest day of the cycle, and his thoughts raced with excitement, *Tonight the* Festival of Light *begins. Grandfather, Francis, and I have been in the woods the entire* Color *quarter. It doesn't seem possible! Surely Francis will return with us to Thistleville today in time to celebrate the first night festivities.*

Zygmunt scrambled down from his perch in a stately pine. Grandfather and Francis had prepared breakfast with cornbread and thistleroot coffee and were talking softly by the fire. They seemed quite serious.

"Grandfather, how soon before we go home? The Festival begins tonight. I can't wait!"

Glancing first at Francis, Chester said, "Son, we must miss the opening night ceremonies. Francis has another plan."

Zygmunt had never missed the Festival. He thought about friends dancing and singing, and the wondrous glow as the beam first appeared. It was awesome! Zygmunt owed everything to his grandfather. Obedience was not easy. It required faith and love.

Daylight would be short. They broke camp and climbed higher on the mountain. The air was crisp and cold. Recognizing a deer trail that led directly to Thistleville, Zygmunt's spirit soared, but Francis ignored it. They continued upward. No one spoke.

As each hour passed, Francis moved faster and without effort. There was a powerful purpose in his stride. As dusk approached, they reached a large plateau with a beautiful stream. Francis broke his strange silence. "We are here! Set your supplies under the trees. Move quickly! We will watch for the beam from the top of the rise where the water flows out from the mountain. Hurry!"

As they rounded a tight curve and caught up with Francis, all were drenched in a pale blue light. Chester and Zygmunt were awestruck. The light grew brighter. They would not see from afar the mysterious beam of the North Star. *No!* Not tonight! They were standing *in* it. But this was impossible! No one ever stood at the end of a rainbow!

All were glowing as if they had become part of the light. Francis stood in the center calm as the night air. He raised his eyes and arms toward the heavens and smiled. "Zygmunt, come here."

Sitting on a boulder just inside the circle of light, Chester savored the scene. It was a proud moment tinged only by the passing realization that he alone remained to see it. As the light grew brighter and warmer, Zygmunt fell to his knees.

"Zygmunt, you have been chosen for a most special mission. Tonight, you become a Seer, the Nobby Master, a role to be played quietly and made manifest in time through your actions.

"This honor comes to you because your singular size and strength are dwarfed only by your unique understanding and compassion for all that live in the Land of the Mitten. You must safeguard the history and knowledge passed to you this night, and you must use the powers given to you in the service of others. You will provide help and leadership for our people now, but your real charge is to protect the past and preserve the future. Let this maxim be your guide:

> *"Intelligence bound by love must rule,*
> *Force cannot sustain.*
> *One engenders vision and harmony;*
> *The other only ignorance and disdain."*

Placing his left hand on Zygmunt's broad shoulders, Francis flicked something into the night air. Tiny particles dancing like sparks from the sun fell all about them. Chester shaded his eyes, blinded momentarily by the brilliance. Francis removed a tattered pouch from his waistcoat and pulled out a small vial. Carefully removing the top, he poured the contents onto Zygmunt's bowed head. Zygmunt's black hair glistened like the deep still waters of a lake drenched in the light of a full moon. Francis placed the upturned palms of his hands over Zygmunt's eyes.

"Zygmunt, Nobbies see with their eyes and speak with their minds. Receive the marks of the Nobby Master: gifts of vision and understanding that grant you power to see even without eyes, and to speak without sound to all that lives. The beam of the North Star is but a symbol of the inner light that must now illumine your path so that others may follow. I bequeath all that I have to you that your light may grow in brilliance and become a beacon to the future. You must carry these gifts of vision and understanding faithfully until it is your time to pass them on to yet another. Do not worry! You will come to know the time and place for this, as I have. Know this as well! As the glow of this Festival fades, so must I. I am the past. Our shared moments here and now are the precious present. You are the future. We await it with great expectation.

Zygmunt, you are the Nobby Master."

Zygmunt and his grandfather stayed with Francis at this sacred place for the duration of the Festival, by the stream at day, and in the circle of light at night. Every second was an added tie to the past, and a key to the future. Zygmunt learned how earlier Nobby Masters taught deer to make trails across meadows and through dense forest by traveling the same paths over and over, trampling down tall grass and brush. These were the pathways used now by wolverines, rabbits, and bobcats trained to carry Nobbies from region to region. Eagles provided emergency passage by day, and the owl served faithfully at night. Great snapping turtles often helped at large ponds. Moles, ferrets, and weasels dug mining shafts, and even ants and beetles helped bring some of the precious gifts of the earth to the surface. Nobbies lived in harmony with nature, thanks to Nobby Masters and their special gifts.

It was with great sadness that Chester and Zygmunt watched the final beam fade, and with it, the gentle Nobby Master named Francis who smiled warmly, embraced both of them, and then walked slowly away into the darkness. They returned to Thistleville—this time to stay. Life in the forest was over; a new life was to begin.

The next few cycles passed quickly. Zygmunt traveled frequently to Nobby villages as far south as the salt mining region of Ogle, and northward to the copper and iron country of Faba. There were few who did not recognize the tall, strong Nobby from Thistleville and his grandfather. Chester remained his guide and mentor. His final wish was granted when Zygmunt met and fell deeply in love with Irene, a beautiful dark-haired Nobbess from the coal mining region of Kora. Their wedding in *Sun* on the longest day of the cycle drew guests from every region. Chester shared their love and companionship until his death in *Harvest* time.

The loss of his grandfather brought an awful emptiness. The ache was deep, much worse than the earlier knot in his stomach. It was a terrible pain. Grandfather had always been at his side, and now he was gone forever—his words, his strength, his wisdom, his love. Withdrawn and depressed, a part of Zygmunt also had died.

Irene's words were simple and direct, "Zygmunt, you can fill the great hole in your heart only by matching every precious memory with a new one. You must live your life to the fullest as he did, not in the past. Memories are to be cherished. They are not meant to cripple or steal away the present or the future."

Holding his hand tightly, Irene led him away from the small knoll at the edge of Thistleville. Grandfather and Francis had given him many tools. It was time to use them. Irene felt a new vigor in his grasp, a powerful surge in his stride. She smiled. He was back. Peace and love ruled in the Land of the Mitten.

## Sons of the Promise

Regions and reality change. It is now twelve cycles later in Thistleville. The tiny village has grown into a center of commerce and art, due in large measure to the tremendous popularity of Zygmunt and Irene throughout all the Nobby regions. But they are alone no more; they are now a family. As all will soon learn, Nobbies are alone no more either! The Land of the Mitten has changed. Something is different!

Lord Norbert paused to sip some water, then began anew.

Zygmunt and Irene had started a tavern and general store shortly after their wedding that served the entire area of Thistleville. Irene sang frequently for tavern guests and always at the *Festival of Light*. She also knew a lot about the healing properties of fruits, flowers, herbs, and spices. Both gave much to Nobby life.

Bo, the firstborn, was now ten. Everyone called him Bo because the brightest rainbow ever seen graced the sky at the moment he was born. He favored his mother in temperament and stature, slight build with very fine features. He read constantly and knew much about nature and animals. His ability to train animals was amazing, as was his knowledge of the seasons and stars. One would have thought that he too had grown up in the woods.

Bo spent many nights high in the arms of a giant blue spruce, gazing in wonder at star fields and shooting stars. Squinting his eyes, he would imagine outlines of animal forms and objects made by the random pattern of the stars. One cycle, he watched mysterious fields of multicolored lights and shapes flash across huge areas in the northern sky. This display lasted for nearly thirty nights. He loved the heavens and the outdoors. Although very athletic, Bo chose to leave the sporting contests of strength and speed to others, especially his younger brother, Theodore, whom he loved, encouraged, and always protected.

Theodore was not the typical younger brother. True, there was a strong resemblance, but at only eight, he already stood as tall as Bo and was much heavier and stronger. Theodore clearly had inherited his father's tremendous physical size, but certainly not his gentle nature. He seemed to look for trouble and always found it. Theodore feared nothing and had to be rescued more than once from an angry badger, porcupine, or skunk. Even then, it was difficult to determine the rescuer as they came running home arm in arm, or laughing with

Bo riding on Theodore's back. They were brothers, best friends, and already a formidable team at school in running, tree climbing, chestnut tossing, and swimming. Theodore trusted Bo and would do anything for him. Bo was his "big" brother and knew just about all there was to know. On the other hand, Bo saw the tremendous size and strength of Theo and even then, recognized that his brother had a heart to match. Oh yes, he was hot-tempered, but never a bully. He became easily frustrated when size and strength alone were not enough to solve a problem—but Bo was always there. They were the sons of Zygmunt and Irene, no doubt about it!

These past twelve cycles had been a time of peace and progress. The regions of Faba, Kora, and Ogle had grown rapidly as Zygmunt trained more animals to help in mining and travel. It also seemed quite natural that tiny Thistleville, the highest location, became the center of all commerce. Many believed this was due more to Zygmunt and Irene than the location. Zygmunt traveled much less now. It truly was a period of peace, one in which both Nobby families and nature prospered. What a great time to be young!

But things never stay the same. Change is a part of life, though not always visible, and often begins long before we notice, just as the seasons begin with subtle changes in temperature and sunlight. As peace had been the hallmark for twelve cycles, turmoil would become the rule in a turbulent and most uncertain time.

"Lord Norbert, what happened? Was there an earthquake? Another forest fire?"

"No, Julia, but a series of events almost as bad."

"What were they?"

Lord Norbert glanced toward the fireplace. "Do you know how late it must be? Look, the logs are ashes again!"

Julia jumped immediately and started a new stack. Again the sparks danced and dipped about her as she piled the logs in crisscross fashion, this time even higher. She poked at the embers, blew at them in short strong bursts, and with a loud puff, flames sprang to life once more. Lord Norbert smiled as Julia returned. In her haste, she had smudged her face. Her green eyes, highlighted now by dark streaks across her delicate cheeks, flashed with excitement. Lord Norbert gently wiped her face with his robe.

"Julia, it's getting very late. Are you sure you want to continue? Perhaps a few days from now…"

"No, Lord Norbert, I would like very much to hear more about Bo and Theodore. I'll be okay, if you're okay."

Lord Norbert patted her head. Her golden hair was as fine and soft as thistle down. He settled back into his chair, closed his eyes for a moment and began.

The *Shiver* season was extremely mild that year. It was the strangest thing. No snow fell before the *Festival of Light* and only about half the normal amount fell throughout the rest of the quarter. *Awakening* came early and with it, a terrible infestation of moths. They spun thick webs in nearly every tree and bush. As millions of hungry young caterpillars emerged in early *Suntime*, they ate their way night and day across huge sections of forest, destroying fruit trees, grape vines, and berry bushes. There was little the Nobbies could do. Only colonies of wasps seemed to prosper. They feasted on the slow moving, fat and defenseless caterpillars, packing their nests with them. This insect infestation placed quite a hardship on those families involved in agriculture, but all survived. Thankfully, this terrible *Suntime* was followed by a very cold *Shiver* season and the moths did not survive.

The following *Awakening*, it seemed like there were two periods named *Rain* instead of one. It got real hot beginning with *Flowers*, and the heat lasted all the way through *Harvest*. It was the hottest *Suntime* anyone could remember, and with the hot sticky air came deer flies. They were terrible! Non-stop buzzing disrupted all of Nobby life. Everyone wore netting outdoors during the day. Again, the wasps prospered. Most work was done in the dark of night while the flies rested. Happily, a severe *Shiver* season followed again and destroyed most of the deer fly larvae.

The next three cycles of *Suntime* were wonderful. Cold *Shiver* quarters helped control the pests. Agriculture and mining flourished. Nobbies traveled freely from region to region, and commerce was the best ever. But again, good fortune did not last. Heavy snows fell throughout the next *Shiver* quarter, followed by rain the entire season of *Awakening*, flooding the swamps and bogs below. Many trails across the great meadows were underwater and impassable. It was at this time that villagers began to report eerie, unfamiliar sounds coming from the bogs. There were other times that travelers heard no noise at all, but felt an eerie presence as if someone, or something, were watching. Animals sensed the danger as well and would bolt to higher ground. Worse, some Nobby travelers were missing. Villagers searched days and nights without finding a single trace. They had vanished like the wind. There was sadness and concern in the land.

Bo and Theodore were fourteen and twelve now, and without doubt, Theodore had inherited his father's stature. They stood eye to eye. The thought of someone threatening Nobbies infuriated Theo. Of course, size and strength figured heavily in his ideas about how to deal with the situation, but Bo and his father knew better. Yes, they must find out who, or what, was making these noises, spying on them, and stealing Nobbies. It must be a smart plan, a foolproof plan, so no one else would get hurt.

Zygmunt enjoyed working with his sons. He was proud to see their concern and enthusiasm, but also concerned about the danger. They were young; Theodore would be thirteen in *Harvest*. For the first time the boys were dealing with an unknown. Always very dangerous! Zygmunt's thoughts raced back to one terrible night long ago, a night of thunder, lightning, and shadows. The sick feeling he had then still haunted his memory. However, his grandfather's reassuring words also remained, "Fear is born in the mind; ignorance gives it life. Learn to see what makes shadows, and fear no more."

Zygmunt knew this lesson applied to strange sounds as well as shadows. The boys didn't. He also knew that this particular unknown made them *all* ignorant—at least for the moment. However, with careful planning it could be a very good learning experience, an opportunity for both of them to grow. Experience is the best teacher, but one must survive to make the lessons worthwhile.

The period of *Sun* had just begun with the longest day. As usual, the celebration outlived the daylight. The Thistleville Tavern, festooned with flowers tied in spectacular yellow and blue bows, rocked with music and laughter. Nobbies from every region danced and sang until morning. Bo and Theodore had a good time, but didn't waste any either. They canvassed the entire tavern gleaning every tidbit about what other Nobbies might have heard, seen, or even felt on the way to Thistleville. They needed clues. Something had to be done and quickly. Thrill of the unknown can be intoxicating.

Eventually the rush of heart-pounding adventure must, however, give way to fatigue. So fight as they might, Bo and Theodore finally surrendered to sleep. It was late afternoon the next day when they awoke. Their father was already meeting with the elders. Final details of a plan were complete.

They entered the room as Zygmunt was explaining, "Since we do not know the source of the strange sounds, we must proceed with extreme caution. Nothing should be done until we know the answer to that question. What to do? I will go ahead alone under cover of darkness. It will be easy for me to enter the bog unseen and unheard. A group would surely be noticed. Once there I will take a high vantage point and signal for the others to follow the next day when the sun reaches its highest point in the midday sky. Understood?

"Bo and Theo, pick ten young Nobbies brave and swift to form a special patrol. Your job is very specific. Come down the mountainside at midday making lots of noise. Come as close as possible to the edge of the swamp, but under *no* circumstance should any of you leave the cover of the fir trees. This is an absolute order! *No matter what!* Bo, do you understand? Whatever or whoever is hidden in the marshes will surely hear the racket, and when they react, I will see them. When I give the signal to retreat, the patrol is to run as fast as possible back to Thistleville. Understood?"

"Okay, but I still think Bo or I should go with you! What if there is a problem? What if you get hurt? We don't want you to go alone!"

"Thank you, Theo! I appreciate and understand your concern, but it is much easier and safer for me to move alone. I will let you know I'm safe. This is a workable plan and the best way to learn the source of these sounds. Once this mystery is solved, we can reassess the situation. We must protect all Nobbies."

The boys reluctantly agreed after the elders told them earlier stories about their father and his amazing powers; something they did not know. So it was set. The action would begin on the evening of the fourth night of *Sun* under the cover of a new moon. Stealth would be the key and darkness the tool used to unlock this mystery.

"I want everyone to get plenty of rest the next two nights. We have much to do. We are dealing with dangerous uncertainties. Mistakes now can be very unforgiving, and we have a great deal to lose."

## The Seed Is Lost

Dark is the evening at four hours past sunset. Town folk gather at the edge of the village. Though the night air is warm, it contains a chill. Irene gives Zygmunt a hug and helps strap a small pack to his back. While spreading soot on his father's forehead and under his eyes to conceal his face even more in the darkness, Theo whispers:

"Take me with you."

Zygmunt smiled, hugged him, and whispered back, "Not this time."

Zygmunt walked over to Bo who was holding the reins of Binder, a favorite wolverine. Standing at least fourteen Thistle leaves high at the shoulders, Binder was the biggest wolverine ever seen. Ever since Zygmunt found him as a young pup with his paws frozen into the swamp, there was a special bond between them. The rescue trip up the mountainside on a makeshift sled of reeds and vines was a feat in itself, one only Zygmunt could have done alone. It took a long time for those big paws to heal, but heal they did with Irene's wisdom and gentle touch. In fact, his paws were bound with bandages and salve for so long, Bo was the one who dubbed him as Binder. Zygmunt and Binder had since logged many miles and moved together as one. Bo signaled his father to come close and whispered something to him, "…not this time."

Zygmunt hugged Bo, mounted Binder, and in an instant, disappeared into the darkness.

No one got much sleep that night. Bo and Theodore paced the tavern floor. It was the longest night in their lives. Theodore knew that Nobbies were peaceful and did not carry weapons, but what about those "things" making the noises and stealing Nobbies? He carefully wrapped a large sharp kitchen knife, and strapped it down the hollow of his back where no one could see it. After all, they were going into the unknown.

The early morning hours were even worse than night. The young Nobby patrol gathered at dawn and together paced the ground waiting until the sun stood directly above, as ordered. It was an endless march, but there was no doubt about the fastest runners when the sun hit its target. They tore down the mountainside, catapulting over rocks and fallen trees, deftly dodging branches and briars. Hearts pounding and lungs burning, they raced

## The Seed Is Lost

down the mountainside toward glory. Pain meant nothing, nor did fear.

As they neared the edge of the tree line, Theodore led Bo by fifty paces. He was glancing backward to assess his lead, when his foot caught a vine. He hit the ground hard. Loose shale sliced into his cheek; a sharp pain burned deep in his left shoulder. Rolling and somersaulting down a steep bank, he dropped hard into a small ravine. When he finally stopped rolling, his fingers found the deep cuts on his face. Oddly, the sight of his own blood was not what bothered him at that moment. It was something else. He was leaning against something strange, yet familiar. A bit dazed, he put out his hand to feel. It was soft, like fur. He turned quickly. No, it couldn't be! How could it be? There was no mistaking! It was Binder. He was dead. Theodore was more stunned from shock than the fall when the others finally caught up.

"What happened?" Bo asked.

"I'm not sure! I tripped and fell. I rolled down the slope right into Binder—and he's dead!"

"Binder? Dead?"

Bo's eyes moved quickly, examining and dissecting each section of ground. Binder was not alone.

There were hornets and parts of hornets scattered all about—all dead. His eyes darted skyward and sure enough, there were several large nests high in a tree. It looked as if his father and Binder had been attacked up on the trail. They probably ran for cover in the ravine. That would explain why Binder lay under the thick thorny branches of a wild hawthorn bush.

"It must have been some battle! Look here, and over there! There are dead hornets everywhere!"

"Keep your voices down," Bo cautioned. "Nests are in the tree right above us."

Cecil, a close friend, whispered, "But where is your father?"

Bo didn't know. He obviously was not there. Bo did know two things, however. First, his father had been caught by surprise and second, wherever he was now, he was unconscious. There was no distress signal. Nothing! Where could he be? Was he even alive? They could only hope. For the first time, Zygmunt's sons and their friends knew and felt the pain that knots the stomach and numbs the senses—*fear*.

On this fateful afternoon fear was not limited to the young Nobby patrol at the base of the mountain. Shortly after they left the village, one of the Nobbies tilling ground accidentally broke open a nest of wasps. The enraged swarm went after everything in sight. Farm animals scampered frantically for the underbrush in the woods. One minute Nobbies were shopping quietly in the

# The Seed Is Lost

village, the next they were screaming in pain inside the tavern. Irene reacted quickly, but knew something was dreadfully wrong. There had been no word from Zygmunt. He knew how she worried.

The tavern was filled with crying and pain; some had been stung several times. Irene grabbed strips of cloth and a large crock of salve, her own blend of thistleseed oil mixed with an extract from animal urine and clay. It was an excellent poultice to draw out venom and to dull pain, but was there enough? Several Nobbesses ran to help. Within a few minutes, it was over.

Irene returned to the counter for a towel to wipe salve from her hands. She thought, *Nobbies here are safe for now. I hope the animals found cover in the woods, but what about tomorrow? Next week? There are just too many wasp and hornet nests this year. Never seen it like this before. Zygmunt would know what to do.*

Irene suddenly raised her hands to her eyes and began to sob.

"...Zygmunt..."

The ravine at the bottom of the mountain was about to become a war zone. Shock and hurt were gone. Theodore was back, his head was clear, and he was mad!

"Bo, where do you think Dad is? Can you pick

up anything? C'mon, you can do it! You've got to! Tell me where he is!"

"I can't! There's nothing! I feel nothing!"

Rage in Theodore's eyes burned wildly as he spoke, "Spread out! Look for signs, anything that might show where my father went!"

Theodore had only whispered the commands, but every syllable was uttered with such force, each echoed off the trees. It seemed that the whole forest heard him. He continued, "Move quietly, the hornets are right above us. But first, come over here!"

Theodore reached back and carefully drew the knife hidden under his shirt. With several heavy blows, he severed thorny branches from the hawthorn bush near Binder handing one to each Nobby, "Stay with a partner. If the hornets return, use these. Stand back to back and swing them around your head and shoulders. It will be difficult for the hornets to sting you without getting ripped by the thorns. Kill as many as you can!"

Hatred shot from his eyes—a frightening sight Bo had never seen before.

As quiet as shadows, they fanned out, eyes straining for the slightest clue. Bo and Theodore climbed back up the steep slope, right to the base of the oak tree holding the nests. They saw nothing. A few hornets buzzed overhead.

## The Seed Is Lost

"No, Theo! We find Dad first, then we'll deal with them!"

Looking back into the ravine, Bo saw the others working the underbrush. It made him sick to see Binder's lifeless body stretched out at the edge of the clearing, head and front legs tucked uselessly into the briars at the base of the hawthorn. *Binder never had a chance,* he thought. *He tried to escape into the briars, but just couldn't make it. He was way too big! Way too big! He never had a chance!*

While Bo was thinking about Binder, Theodore picked up a rock and hurled it at the nearest nest. It missed. Bo grabbed his arm and as hard as he could push, moved in unison with Theo toward the edge of the ravine. They started down, but along different paths. Vines and underbrush were very dense. Theo's knife was busy. Their eyes strained for signs, anything like a snapped limb or piece of clothing. Bo's mind wandered again. He didn't know why, but something was not right. What was it? What was he missing?

As they neared the bottom, Bo moved faster. He didn't know why. *Where would Father go? Would he ever leave Binder alone with the hornets? Why did Binder pick the smallest briar clump in the open as a sanctuary? He couldn't even fit under that bush! Why...* Half running and falling, Bo raced the rest of the way down the slope and ran across the clearing. He yelled for the others.

"Theo, grab Binder's hind legs! C'mon, everyone! Grab a hold! Hurry! *Pull!* Pull as hard as you can! All together! Pull! Pull!"

The veins in Theodore's neck looked as if they would explode. Slowly, Binder's body moved from under the briars, and as it did, Bo saw the tips of his father's boots. He was lying in the space between Binder's huge front paws and his neck. His father's jacket was clenched in Binder's teeth.

"Pull harder! Quick! Dad is under Binder! He's breathing! Theo, he's alive!"

Theodore joined Bo, and together pulled their father into the open. But tug as they might, they could not free the jacket from Binder's jaws. Two strokes of the blade against the jacket did. Bo checked his father. Face and arms were terribly swollen, there was no telling how many times he had been stung. Breathing was slow and difficult, his eyes were rolled back and his skin was clammy. Bo knew these were bad signs. Time was now the enemy. His father had to be carried home before the poison completely paralyzed his heart and lungs.

"Theo, there's no time for a stretcher! Can you carry him? We'll clear the way and help you as much as we can. Hurry! We must get him to Mom. There's not much time!"

In one powerful motion, Theodore swung his father across his shoulders and moved toward the slope.

## The Seed Is Lost

Bo wrapped a rope around Theo's waist and gave the ends to John and James, two brothers who were their closest friends. "Climb quickly and stay ahead of him! Pull him! Don't let him fall!"

The others were already marking and clearing his path. Zygmunt's life depended on speed. Bo followed with his hand in the small of Theo's back. He closed his eyes for a moment to allow his thoughts to race ahead to Thistleville, the tavern, and to his mother.

# Binder's Trail

Nobbies fill the tavern. Zygmunt is in an upstairs bedroom. Members of the Nobby patrol, exhausted from the frantic climb, are resting at tables. The room is filled with concerned neighbors and questions. Bo and Theodore enter the hall and walk toward their friends. Bo reaches for an outstretched cup of tea, takes a sip, and continues alone to the front of the room. It is very quiet. Bo glances quickly at Theodore and begins:

"Thank you for your concern. Dad is extremely weak but conscious and breathing a bit easier. Mom wrapped him in one big bandage, and he's drinking special herbal teas. He'll be okay, thanks to Theo's strength and the grit of our patrol friends. We are forever grateful.

"You want to know what happened. So do we! It's not clear, but we can piece some things together. Dad and Binder were moving along the main trail toward the base of the mountain. As they neared the end of the tree line, a swarm of hornets attacked. We don't know why. It's most unusual for hornets to fly at night. Apparently, Dad rode Binder off the trail to the side of a ravine looking for cover. Binder must have stumbled and both went tumbling. Unfortunately, the bottom of the ravine had a large clearing instead of underbrush affording scant protection and no escape. My father remembers only that he and Binder fought the hornets for a very long time then he must have passed out.

"When Theo led us down the mountain, he tripped and fell into the same ravine. That move was not planned! Whether by luck or providence, I know not. But if not, our father certainly would have died. The battle with hornets was evident. Insect body parts were all over the clearing. What was not evident, however, was how the struggle ended—until now.

"When my father passed out, Binder must have grabbed him by the waistcoat and dragged him to the safety of that small briar bush. There was not enough room for both of them. It appears that Binder pushed him as far as he could under the bush. Then he covered Dad with his own body. Binder was unprotected and at the mercy of the hornets. They showed none and stung him until he died. This is how we found them—together. As you know, the bond between Dad and Binder was very special; even more so now. We plan to return to the ravine tomorrow to provide a proper burial."

An elderly Nobby broke the uneasy silence, "Did you see anything? Did you hear anything?"

Theodore answered from the table, "No, we saw and heard nothing. We didn't get close enough, but we will the next time! That's a promise! First, however, we must deal with the wasps and hornets!"

The gathering at the tavern broke up quickly as Nobbies scampered to spread the word about the hornet attack and how the great wolverine named Binder had saved Zygmunt's life. Theodore remained at the table with the patrol to talk about the return trip to bury Binder. Without a word, Bo left the dining hall through a side door and quickly disappeared into his workshop at the rear of the tavern. He needed quiet, a place to think…a plan. The hornets and wasps were deadly. How to contain them and drive them away—or destroy them—without anyone else getting hurt? There were so many!

During the past two cycles his dad had talked often in the workshop about a wonderful old Nobby named Francis. One particular story kept coming back. Francis had said that mining was not only the source of Nobby wealth, but that it also held secrets that one day would give rise to a kingdom. Bo scratched his head, "What secrets?" He and his father talked about salt, gold, silver, iron, lead, and coal. No secrets here!

"Come to think of it, there was something found some time ago in Kora, a clear rock-like substance that looked like salt, but was not. Some pieces were large and rough, others small and smoother, and some of the same material was simply like grains of sand. What was this material? What did it do? How could it be used?"

Bo locked the door, lit a thistle-oil lamp, and drew covers over the windows. His eyes darted for just a moment toward the upper bedroom and his father. He walked to a cupboard, carefully removed several pieces of this strange substance and went to work. It was late afternoon.

Irene continued to change the dressings on Zygmunt's wounds every three hours. The fever was gone. Feeling was returning slowly to his arms and legs. His face was the worst. His eyes were swollen shut, but breathing was much easier, and his voice a bit stronger. As she replaced a moist compress over his eyes, she felt a chill: "Another few minutes…it would have been too late."

"Irene, is everyone okay?"

"Yes, Zygmunt, everyone is fine. You're home. We are all safe."

"Where are Bo and Theo?"

"Both are downstairs in the dining hall."

"Irene, make sure they stay away from the hornets! Something is wrong! The hornets cannot be controlled! They're very dangerous!"

"Don't worry, I'll talk to them. Lay back. Get some rest."

Zygmunt's words were very disturbing. Something was dreadfully wrong if he could not control the hornets. He was right too about the boys. They must stay away from the hornets until he was well enough to figure out what was wrong. By the looks of his face, it would be awhile.

It was early evening now. Bo skipped supper. Both Theo and his mother had knocked at the door asking him to eat, but he refused saying, "I'm fine! I'm not hungry, I'll eat later. Come back in two hours." They didn't know what he was doing, but they knew Bo. When he focused on something, it was best to leave him alone. He was just like his father.

Bo was sure this strange substance did hide a secret, but what? He needed more time. As he studied several of the larger samples, he noted two things: they were not as heavy as they looked, and they were extremely hard. He tried several times to break them or to cut off a jagged piece, but nothing would even scratch the surface. The same was true for the smaller pieces.

When he placed samples under a brighter light to see them better, something amazing happened. They reflected the light, but it became many different colors coming from different points inside. They were tiny shafts of light, very bright and brilliant, and changed in color when he turned the material to a different angle to the light. Bo had never seen anything like it. His heart began to beat a bit faster with these new discoveries, but what good was the information? It didn't help solve the hornet problem.

"Bo, it's Theo! Are you still in there?"

"Yes, I'm here. Everything is okay!"

"It's getting very late. In fact, it's nearly midnight. Are you almost finished? Mom is concerned and wants you to eat and rest."

"I'm fine. Tell Mom I'm not hungry; I'll eat later. I'm working on something and I can't quit just now. I've got to keep going!"

"Can I help you? Open the door! I'll sit with you!"

"Thank you, Theo, but I need to think about this by myself. I'll call you as soon as I find what I'm looking for. I promise!"

Theo went to the upstairs room. His mother continued to change the bandages on his father's eyes. "Did Bo stop for the night?"

"No! He said to tell you he was fine. He is not hungry and does not want to quit right now."

"What is he doing?" Zygmunt asked.

"I don't know. He didn't say. He did promise to come and get me when he found what he was looking for.

Don't worry, Dad, he's fine."

Bo was certain this strange, hard material held an answer for the hornets, but if it did, the answer was certainly far from certain. It was a feeling though, a very strong feeling. He just needed more time. He forgot hunger and felt no fatigue. His focus was so intense, he saw and heard nothing but the strange rocks and his own thoughts. Theo's pounding at the door two hours later went unnoticed and unanswered.

Bo spent a long time just thinking as he held and turned the various specimens under the light. While the multicolored reflections were amazing and beautiful, his thoughts began to stray from light to the other noticeable quality, hardness. He rubbed two together and saw that one actually scratched the other. That was interesting because nothing else could even make the slightest mark. He began to bang the rocks together, striking them harder and harder. Nothing! Just as he was about to stop, one of them broke in half, cut as cleanly as with a knife. Bo was puzzled. He couldn't explain it, but made a note in his log. It was at that moment when a simple question crossed his mind, *If the rocks are so hard, what are the small grains like?* There were several sacks of this "sand" in the corner behind his father's workbench. He moved quickly. Curiosity is a great motivator.

As he emptied one of the smaller sacks onto the table, he noted that this sand was very similar to regular sand, but the grains were not all exactly the same size. He grabbed a handful, sifting it gently through his fingers. He did it again, and again, feeling the grains with his fingers and his mind. Yes, they were not all the same, but they were hard, very hard. Some were also sharp. Bo rubbed his eyes with the backs of his hands. Cradling his head in his arms, he rested at the table for just a few moments. Startled by his own thoughts, he leapt to his feet knocking the chair across the room, "What if…? Yes! Why not…? Yes! It should work!"

Bo moved with new vigor to the sacks of sand…to the storage room for a small jar…to the cupboard for a large pot…to a barrel just outside the rear door, and then back to his workbench. He moved quickly and quietly, but his thoughts were loud and clear, and racing far ahead. If what he had in mind worked, he would be ready by dawn to go with Theo and the others back down the mountain. They would deal first with the hornets, and then bury Binder. This must be done!

After taking a scoop of pine tar resin from the barrel and placing it in the large pot, he began slowly to thin it with thistleseed oil. This would be the test.

"Yes, it worked!"

The mixture became thinner, almost like gravy, but stayed very sticky. Bo added a bit more oil, then, slowly mixed in some of the sand. He took a small feather brush and spread the mixture on the underside of a tiny reed basket. After just a few minutes in the open air, the coating became rock hard, yet stayed as sticky as the pure pine resin.

Bo could hardly keep from shouting, he was so excited! But this was not the time to celebrate; that would come tomorrow evening. Much needed to be done before daybreak.

Just as dawn pierced the darkness, Theo darted from his room. The chill in the air breathed new life into all of his senses. A dazzling white frost cloaked the land. The weariness from the past two days was gone. He had met secretly with members of the patrol to plan a dawn trip down the mountain before anyone awoke. His mother's words still echoed in his ears, "I want to see you and Bo later. Your father asked me to talk to you both about the hornets." Theo knew exactly what she wanted to say. "Stay away from the hornets! Do not go back down the mountain!" As he moved silently toward the workshop, he smiled. *You can't disobey your mother if you can't hear her!* The door to the workshop was open. This was a good sign.

"Theo, come in! Have the others arrived yet? We must move quickly before Mom shows up!"

"We agreed to meet on the trail just outside the village. I'm sure they're already waiting for us. Are you ready?"

Bo pointed to three buckets, rope, a sack of

hollowed-out gourds, and a strange looking costume on the workbench. "Grab two buckets! Let's go! I'll explain on the way!"

The troop was waiting with shovels, ropes, and clubs. They began moving as soon as Bo and Theo appeared in the trees. John and James stayed back to join them, and then followed the others down the trail. This too would be a quick trip. As before, strict silence was the rule. Nearing the bottom of the tree line, they moved more cautiously. The hornets were close, but the strange presence in the swamp was still a mystery. They needed no more surprises. Better to deal with one problem at a time. Bo knelt, waved everyone closer, and whispered,

"It's very early and cool. If we're lucky, all the hornets are still in their nests. We must disable them before burying Binder. The noise of our shovels would irritate them, and we'd all be under attack. I've made a special glue to spread over each nest. This must be done quickly, carefully, and without a sound. We must trap all the hornets in their own nests. There is not much time.

"Theo, I know you want to be the one who climbs the tree. Put your head through the hole in this blanket and wear it like a robe. Tie this rope around your waist. Also, put on dad's old hat. It has netting attached to protect your face. Everything has been coated with another mixture; James and John, help Theo. We'll go ahead and get the ropes and buckets ready. No noise!"

Bo and the others moved quietly to the base of the old oak. So far, so good. There were no hornets. Spreading out in teams, they coiled ropes and gently flung them over the limbs closest to each nest. They were ready. Still no hornets. Theo was ready too. As he neared the base of the tree, Bo handed him some small pieces of cloth.

"When you get near each nest, pour glue around the opening first and slap one of these patches over the hole. You don't need very much. The glue is very strong and sticky. As fast as you can pour glue over the patch and then all over the rest of the nest. Start at the top and let it drip down. Be careful! Climb as fast as you can from one nest to the next. We will hoist the glue to you in the gourds. Pour as fast as you can. Drop the gourds when you're done and go to the next nest. Theo, remember! You must cover the opening first!"

Theo began his climb. Still no hornets.

When Theo reached the lowest nest, he glanced down. He could see Binder's body in the ravine. Anger returned. The veins in his neck swelled with rage. His eyes darted across the ground and there was Bo, right below, motioning him to be calm and quiet. Bo was right! He was always right. Theo reached for the gourd dangling near his feet, removed the plug, and crawled slowly to the opening of the first nest. He saw and heard nothing as he poured around the hole and patted the patch into place. He stood up and in just a matter of seconds, doused the entire nest, dropped the empty gourd, and was gone.

Theo returned to the central trunk and climbed to the next ring of limbs. Two nests were at this level, but on opposite sides of the tree. He moved first to the larger nest that hung right over the trail. It was furthest from the ravine and probably the one holding the hornets that first attacked his father. It was a long crawl to the nest because it hung way out near the end of the limb. He moved with the stealth and sureness of a cat, eyes frozen on the prey. Again, he took the gourd swinging silently at his feet, cradled it gingerly in his hands, and crawled toward the opening. This was a bigger nest.

When Theo stood, his eyes were even with the opening, but the nest hung from a smaller and higher branch. It was difficult to reach the nest because it swung out and away from the limb where he stood. The rising sun was beginning to warm the morning air, however, and there was no time for second attempts. He opened the gourd, splashed Bo's mixture around the hole, and pressed a patch over it. He had no problem pouring the glue down the front and sides of the nest, but could not reach the back. As Bo and the others watched in amazement, Theo leapt to the branch where the nest hung and grabbed it with his left arm. While dangling in mid air, he emptied the rest of the gourd over the back of the nest, dropped it to the ground, and swung back down to the larger limb. Had they not seen it, they would not have believed it. Without even looking, he ran along the limb back to the trunk, slid around it to the other side, and moved toward the next nest hanging over the ravine. A low hum was coming now from the closed nests, but only Theo could hear it. Time was running out.

Experience is the best teacher, and Theo was a fast learner. In no time at all, he secured the third nest, but just barely. He saw movement inside the opening as he sealed it. The hum was getting louder now. He looked below. James and John had climbed to the lower limbs and were pointing toward the coated nests. They could hear the hum. Theo ran along the limb back to the center trunk. His foot slipped and he fell, face first, but the limb was wide enough to catch him. The impact, however, reopened the cut on his cheek. He got up and ran again. The blood tickled as it dripped down the side of his face.

The last nest was quite a bit higher and on the backside of the tree. As he climbed higher up the trunk to get into position, a lone hornet flew out of the opening. Bo saw it, too. Theo didn't care. He moved methodically out along the new limb, but this time there was no crawling. He remained on his feet. Again, the opening of the nest was at eye level. Another hornet flew out. And another. In all, he guessed about a dozen. None saw him. He grabbed the final gourd and moved right in front of the hole. Another hornet flew out, narrowly missing his head. This one saw him. Defiantly, Theo stood erect and splashed the glue all around the hole. He doused the next two hornets that came out as well. Slamming the patch over the hole, he leaned against it with his shoulder to keep other hornets inside from pushing it away. As he did, the gourd fell to the ground. He could feel the angry hornets striking the cloth, but they were no match for him and the glue. It held; so did he.

A second gourd was on the way up when he felt the first hornet strike him in the back. Thanks to Bo, there was no sting. Theo bent forward, reached up over his left shoulder and pulled off its head. Its twitching body bounced off the limb and then fell to the ground. The noise from the nests was now a loud buzz. Everyone could hear it.

Theo grabbed the new gourd just sent from below, but did not separate it from the rope. Clasping an overhead branch, he swung to the top of the nest. He stood right on it. The buzzing was very loud now and the nest vibrated under his feet. As he poured the glue all around, a second hornet flew directly at his chest. Theo saw him coming. One swipe with his left arm knocked it to the top of the nest. Bo's glue did the rest. He could feel the fury below inside the nest. Several others struck at the same time and Theo fell to his knees. John and James were attacked, as well, but managed to drop to the ground unharmed. Theo rolled sideways kicking one hornet into the side of the nest, swatted a second into the glue with his left hand, and crushed a third with his right. As he threw this last hornet into the side of the nest, two others struck from above. They met a similar fate. Theo reached for the gourd and continued coating the entire nest and everything on it. When he finished, he dropped the gourd, raised his arms and screamed, "That's for Dad and Binder!" Everyone yelled and danced around the base of the tree. No one heard or cared about the buzzing any more. The glory and joy of the moment left quickly, however, as their thoughts turned to the ravine and Binder. It was time to repay a debt.

Theo hated the ravine. It was and would always remain a place of death. No one argued when he suggested moving Binder. With a makeshift sled, they carried him up the slope to the base of the great oak tree. All buzzing from above had ceased. Their silence was a fitting tribute, but certainly not an even swap. Bo picked a spot near the trail just a few paces from the base of the tree. The digging would be easier. Only the occasional ring of a shovel hitting stone disturbed the silence.

After wrapping Binder's head carefully in the blanket Theo had just worn in the tree, Bo signaled the patrol to lower his body into the grave. In a soft, faltering voice, Bo thanked the great wolverine for his friendship, devotion, and loyalty. Binder had certainly repaid his father for saving his life as a pup. Each sprinkled a handful of dirt over the open grave, and then covered it. With a final salute, the patrol placed a large boulder at the head of the grave. Theo once again reached to the hollow of his back. Climbing the oak, he carved where all could see: "Binder's Trail."

It was mid-afternoon when everything was completed. Bo closed his eyes for a moment to let his mother know they were fine and on the way home. In all the excitement, no one had noticed the eyes peering from the tall reeds at the edge of the bog.

"Julia, are you okay? Julia!"

"Yes, Lord Norbert, I'm fine. I was just thinking about Binder, Irene and Zygmunt, and Bo and Theo. I had no idea what life was like in those early days. In fact, I never knew much about our ancestors or history. They were certainly brave. I can almost see them. Actually, I feel as though I know them. What happened next? You must tell me! Please!"

"But Julia, it's nearly three o'clock in the morning! It's your birthday! You're going to be too tired to celebrate if you don't get some rest. Relatives and friends from all over the kingdom are coming to see you. We can talk more later. Rest for a while!"

"I know. Today will be very busy, but I can't sleep now. I'm just too excited! I've got to know more. Everyone else is sleeping; they won't know we talked all night. Oh, I'm sorry! How selfish! I'm thinking only about myself! You must be very tired, Lord Norbert. Here I am, keeping you up all night! I'm sorry! "

"Don't feel bad, Julia, I've enjoyed every minute. I couldn't sleep either. I'm also very excited! Let's make a deal! I'll tell you as much as I can about Thistledom before the sun peeks in the east window. When the sunlight hits the floor, I will stop, and you must promise to lie down and rest, even if you don't sleep. Agreed?"

"Okay," Julia laughed, "but you must also promise to talk as fast as you can! What happened when Bo and Theo returned home?"

Lord Norbert nodded his head, smiled as he ruffled her hair, and stared quietly for a moment at the dwindling fire to gather his thoughts. He had been talking so much, he no longer felt the night chill of *Colors*. He loosened his robe a bit and then settled back into his chair. There was still so much to tell her, so much for her to know. He continued.

It was a triumphal return. The tavern swelled to capacity to hear about Bo's special glue and Theo's bravery. News about Binder's Trail also met loud applause. There was much to celebrate, but only briefly. Bo and Theo learned that their father had suffered permanent damage from the venomous attack. His eyesight was bad and nerve damage in his legs made it impossible to walk without assistance. They were heartsick. Zygmunt, however, was not. He called a family meeting that evening to remind them that he had survived the hornets, he was alive and well, and that there was too much to do to waste time feeling sick or sorry. Irene would be his eyes, Theo his legs, and Bo his hands. Together as a family, they would move forward; so would Thistleville. And so they did.

Bo made more glue and the special coating for clothes. Over the last few weeks of *Color*, and then throughout the next seasons of *Awakening* and *Suntime*, Theo and the Nobby Patrol traveled everywhere to destroy hornet and wasp nests. The fame of Zygmunt's family grew, especially Theo's feats of strength and daring.

Life in Thistleville went well for the next two and a half cycles. Bo continued his experiments with those wondrous rocks, learning more and more about them. Working with his father, he also designed better training programs for the many animals and birds used in Nobby travel and commerce. Theo continued to visit all the regions working closely with village elders to organize community councils and to improve roads and major trails. Bo noticed that Theo spent a lot of time in the salt mining region of Ogle. A young Nobbess named Astrid lived there. He had not met her yet, but he knew she was very special. Theo talked about her long red hair, fair skin, soft green eyes, and lilting voice. Theo said, "She's terrific and her father is head of the Council of Elders!" Bo knew she was very special, and so was Theo.

Irene and Zygmunt also enjoyed a time of peace and happiness during this period. They saw the entire Nobby community responding to the leadership of their sons. This was a time of great progress; they were very proud. But, as *Color* approached, Zygmunt began to spend long hours alone. Bo had devised a small three-wheeled cart that gave him greater independence and mobility. Frequently, he would ride alone into the woods at sunrise and return just before dusk. Irene was concerned at first, but then realized that the woods had been his first real home. Zygmunt was happy there. He needed the space and time to think. With the arrival of *Wind*, trips to the woods gave way to long hours in his study on the top floor at the rear of the tavern. Here the trees outside the windows gave him the same sense of oneness with nature, but without the bite of the cold north wind. Irene knew something weighed heavily on his mind, but he said nothing and she would not pry. When he was ready, he would tell her.

He always did.

    Soon it was *Snow* and the *Festival of Light* was near. Excitement filled the Land because the *Festival*, once again, would last for three full days and nights. This cycle marked another special occasion because Council Elders from all the regions were coming to celebrate together in Thistleville for the first time. Theo worked hard on the plans for lodging, meals, and special events, and not without good reason. A certain young Nobbess from Ogle was also coming to Thistleville.

    Bo stayed quietly in the background. He loved to watch Theo in action. It was amazing how he moved with such confidence, set priorities, solved problems, and got everyone to work so well together. Bo's chest swelled almost as large as Theo's when he heard people speak in such glowing terms about his younger brother. Bo saw clearly the coming changes in his brother's life, but he could not know the tremendous change about to occur in his own.

    It was the day before the Shortest Day. Guests were already arriving. The tavern became the control center for festival activities. Theo had everything in order. It was shortly after lunch when Irene whispered to Bo that his father wanted to see him in the study. Bo excused himself from conversation with elders from Kora and climbed the steps to the third floor. He knocked softly and entered the room.

"Bo, I have a favor to ask."

"What is it, Dad? Say it and it's yours."

"The *Festival* lasts three days and nights. I want to be here for the first two days and nights. In the late morning of the third day, I would like you to set up the large sled with our best team of wolverines. Your mother and I will be ready."

"Okay, but where are we going? Will we miss the closing ceremonies? Mom always sings at them!"

"I know, but there is something I must do, and I need both of you."

Bo was puzzled by the strange request and the unfamiliar tone in his father's voice. This was certainly an unexpected development. As Bo shook his head in agreement, Zygmunt raised his hand.

"And Bo, don't say anything about this to your mother or brother. It must remain between us for the moment. I'll explain later. Agreed?"

Now Bo really was uneasy. He and Theo had no secrets. *What was this all about?*

# No One Stands at the End of the Rainbow

One minute there is rain and sleet, the next, it's dusk on the night of the Shortest Day. Everyone is in the large clearing at the north side of the tavern. From here, there is a perfect view of the beam. Musicians are in tune, dancers poised, and the food is ready. It's amazing to see how many different costumes there are in the black, green, and white colors of *Snow*. Zygmunt and Irene are on the side porch holding hands. Theo and Astrid are at the front edge of the clearing. Every eye is set on the North Star, except two. Bo is standing on the ground out of sight at the edge of the porch. He is watching his father.

Zygmunt held Irene close with eyes fixed on the beam. It was only a faint thread connecting the heavens and the earth. No matter how many times one saw this mysterious glow sever the blackness of night, it remained an awesome sight. Bo glanced momentarily at the beam and then back to his parents. The stream of light slowly grew in intensity, as did the excitement. Singing and dancing, the crowd in the clearing joined hands to form a big circle around Theo and Astrid. It was opening night of a three-night super celebration of light. Snow was falling in huge, puffy flakes already erasing the ground. What could be better? Bo watched as his parents swung slowly on their swing, the warm glow of the distant beam softly lighting their faces. They were deep in conversation and very happy. Unseen, Bo moved from the porch through the shadows to join the celebration. As he turned away, Zygmunt pointed to the distant brilliant spot on the mountain. Surprise filled Irene's face. Both stood, stretched briefly in the crisp night air, and then hand in hand, retired to their private chambers.

The party went nonstop throughout the next day and night. So did the snowfall. Everything was just perfect! The Festival was truly a feast for the eyes, stomach, and the spirit. There were contests of strength and skill in skiing, logging, tree climbing, and sledding. Young Nobbesses vied for honors with an endless array of pies, cookies, happyday strudels, and special breads. There were dance ensembles, choirs, and costume competitions, something for everyone. It was the best Festival ever, thanks to Theo!

In the Nobby calendar, this was a fourth cycle so the beam would indeed shine even brighter for a third extra night. Zygmunt recalled fondly that Festival spent with Francis and his grandfather some twenty-four cycles earlier. That too had been a special three-day celebration. He remembered everything, especially the words of Francis:

*The beam of the North Star is but a symbol of the inner light that must now illumine your path that others may follow. I bequeath all that I have to you that your light may grow in brilliance and become a beacon to the future. You must carry these gifts faithfully until it is your time to pass them on. Do not worry! You will come to know the time and place, as I have.*

Zygmunt lay quietly in bed, his thoughts reliving the past. Francis was right about his knowing the time and place someday. Zygmunt's smile was hidden by the early morning darkness. The final day of the Festival had arrived. It was time! He knew the place. Now for sure, he knew the face. He rose quietly in the early morning darkness, kissed Irene softly on the cheek, and left the chamber.

Nobbies filled the tavern for breakfast. Such excitement! Today would bring finals in all the competitions. Prizes! A fabulous costume parade would begin the early evening celebration lit by the beam itself. Finally, the *Festival of Light Ball* beginning with a grand march led by the Council of Elders would cap the festivities. Theo had worked very hard. The success was his. The Council of Elders would honor him later at a midday luncheon. The family shared a private breakfast upstairs. Theo invited Astrid. Zygmunt and Bo stood as both entered the room. Irene smiled warmly:

"Good morning, Astrid! Welcome to our home!"

"Thank you! It's very lovely. I'm happy to be here!"

Theo held Astrid's chair as she sat down.

Breakfast was great! They laughed and told stories. Bo did a few magic tricks. Theo talked about a growing interest in establishing a Central Council of Elders to administer major Nobby issues like education, transportation, commerce and safety throughout all the regions. After Theo spoke, they all clapped and teased him. His enthusiasm was contagious. It was one of his greatest strengths.

"Son, you've done a terrific job organizing the Festival! Your mother and I are very proud. I know your work with the Council of Elders is most important for the future. This is an important time in our history and this is going to be a very busy day—for all of us. You've got many things to do as the Festival comes to a close, but there is something most important that I must do today, as well. I have asked Bo to take your mother and me on a short trip."

"Where are you going? Will you be back in time for the luncheon?"

"No, Theo, we will not return until tomorrow afternoon. Please represent me at the luncheon."

"Where are you going? Why must you leave today?"

"I can't tell you right now. This is something I must do, and I must do it today. It's very important!"

"I'll go with you!"

"No, Theo, you must tend to matters here. Bo will take care of us."

Theo looked at Bo for some clue, but all Bo could do was shrug his shoulders. He knew no more than Theo. As they rose from the table, Theo asked his father, "Will you tell me about this later?"

Zygmunt smiled, "You will understand it all later. Cover for me!"

Bo brought the sleigh to the rear entrance of the tavern. Zygmunt and Irene slipped out the door, got into the rear seat, and Bo headed across the clearing to the trail leading north up the mountain. The Festival continued in town. The luncheon of Council Elders was about to begin. No one saw them leave.

The sleigh continued northward up a winding trail for several hours. The wolverines kept a steady pace. Occasionally, Zygmunt spoke briefly to Irene, but Bo couldn't make it out. The trail was new and unfamiliar. He looked back, and his father motioned him to continue straight ahead.

They continued for another hour. It was late afternoon and sunlight was quickly fading. The trail led through a dense stand of firs and pines. There was little underbrush and it was much darker, almost like a tunnel. As they emerged, his father told him to take the path to the right. Bo stopped the sleigh because he couldn't see a path. His father pointed toward a rock formation. Bo turned the sleigh and continued. Yes, there was a pathway, but it was barely visible in the snow. It was also quite steep, leading almost directly up the side of the mountain. The wolverines strained at their harnesses. As they passed the rock formation, Bo heard running water. Nightfall was just minutes away. Darkness didn't bother him, but the cold air did. They approached a sharp turn in the trail, and as they rounded the corner, it opened onto a large plateau with a stream flowing out of the mountain. Zygmunt smiled, waved his arms happily over his head.

"We are here! Pull the sleigh over there in the trees by the stream. We must move quickly! We will watch for the beam of the North Star from the top of the rise just on the other side of the crevice—over there where the water flows out from the mountain. We must hurry!"

With Bo and Irene's help, they moved toward the rise. Zygmunt thought how natural those same long-forgotten words of Francis had suddenly come to his own lips. "We must hurry!" Now he understood the strange urgency that had fired Francis' spirit that evening so long ago. He felt as though the old gentle Nobby Master was again there with him. Perhaps he was. Surprisingly, Zygmunt let go and began to walk slowly to the center of what looked like a large stage with a slate floor. There was no snow on it. Bo and his mother stayed at the edge leaning against a large boulder. Bo had turned to talk to his mother when the beam suddenly appeared. They were awestruck! There was his father, arms and eyes raised toward the heavens, standing tall in a pale blue light. They couldn't believe their eyes! As they watched in amazement, the beam grew and began to engulf them as well.

"This must be a dream! This is impossible! It's an illusion!"

Their skin glowed as if they had become part of the beam. Bo and his mother began to realize how special this night was, but still did not understand why they were there.

"Bo, come here."

Irene sat down on the boulder just inside the lighted circle. Her eyes followed every movement. It was the most glorious sight she had ever seen. The light grew even brighter and she felt its soothing warmth. She watched intently as Bo approached his father.

"Bo, I am so pleased that you are the one. This moment was beyond my wildest dreams. I never expected you would be the one chosen to follow me. Tonight in the special radiance and power of this third-night beam, you are to become a Nobby Seer—the new Nobby Master. As of old, your role is to be played humbly and made manifest in time only through your actions. This singular honor comes to you because of your uncommon wisdom, patience, selfless nature, and inexhaustible charm. You inherit a great legacy of history and knowledge that is yours alone to safeguard, along with special powers to be used only in the service of others. You are to provide critical leadership to our Nobby world now, but as is true for each Nobby Master, your real charge is to protect its past while preserving its future. This is our guide:

> *Intelligence bound by love must always rule,*
> *force cannot sustain.*
> *One engenders vision and harmony;*
> *The other only ignorance and disdain.*

"Kneel, my son."

Zygmunt's left hand trembled as he placed it on Bo's shoulder. Fine powder once again danced and glittered like sparks from the sun. As Chester had done before, Irene shaded her eyes, blinded momentarily by the dazzling display. She watched intently as Zygmunt reached in his waistcoat and pulled out a tattered old pouch. Strange. She had never seen it before. He withdrew a small vial, carefully removed the stopper, and poured the contents onto Bo's bowed head. His black hair glistened, reflecting the light of the beam like a piece of polished coal. Bo's head remained bowed as Zygmunt placed the upturned palms of his hands against his son's eyes.

"Bo, receive the marks of the Nobby Master; gifts of vision and understanding that grant you the power to see without eyes and to speak without sound to all that lives. The beam of the North Star is but a symbol of the inner light that must now illumine your path that others may follow. I bequeath all that I have to you that your light may grow in brilliance and become a beacon to the future. You must carry these gifts faithfully until it is your time to pass them on. Do not worry! You will come to know the time and place as I have. As the light beam fades away, so in time must we all. I am the past. The moments we share now are the present. You are the future. Your mother and I await it with great expectation. We will share it with you for as many more beams as he who set the North Star in place shall grant. You are the Nobby Master. We are very proud and shall never forget this night."

Tears welled from Irene's eyes and flowed down her cheeks like rivulets of pure sunlight. She knew very well that her presence was not needed for this sacred ceremony. Zygmunt simply had chosen to share it with her. Their lives had become one in service. Their separate talents were so beautifully combined and visible in both Bo and Theo. Zygmunt and Irene were indeed but a single spirit drawing life from two hearts. She moved gracefully to center stage, embracing her son and kissing her husband. They remained together within the warmth and protection of the beam until it faded in the glory of a new sunrise, and the coming of a new day.

The town was still bustling with visitors. Theo was anxiously waiting alone at the rear of the tavern when the sleigh emerged from the woods. Bo waved and Theo smiled. He grabbed the reins in his big powerful hands as the sleigh came to a stop.

"Is everything okay?" he asked.

"Perfect!" they responded in unison.

Theo had never seen them so happy.

"How are things here?" Bo asked.

"Perfect! I asked Astrid to marry me, and she said, '*Yes!*'"

"A wedding!" Julia blurted. "This is wonderful! What a story! I love weddings! Please tell me all about it! Everything! *Please?*"

Lord Norbert laughed. It was good to see Julia so excited, so animated. "Julia, there isn't enough time tonight to tell you all about the wedding. I'll never finish the rest of the story before sunrise. It's impossible!"

Julia's face could not hide her disappointment. Lord Norbert came quickly to the rescue. "Okay! I'll give you just a quick overview now and I will tell you *all* the details later. I promise! Okay?"

She managed a smile and nodded. Lord Norbert gave her a love tap on the cheek and continued.

Theodore and Astrid were married later that cycle in the period of *Sun* at sunrise on the Longest Day. The celebration was larger even than the *Festival of Light*. Thistleville was bursting at the seams with tents stretched from the side of the tavern all the way to the edge of the forest.

Astrid wore a long delicate wedding gown that looked as though it were sewn from snowflakes. Her veil of white lace was spun from thread as fine as spider's silk. Theodore, stretching to his full height, stood tall and proud—as handsome a Nobby as you will ever see. Guests wore their finest fashions resplendent in the blue, yellow, pink, and white colors of the season. Bo did the honors as his brother's Sponsor at the wedding, and later as Master of Ceremonies at the daylong celebration. Zygmunt and Irene were so happy. The beam in their eyes was reminiscent of another beam they had shared not too long ago. Irene wrote a song and sang it herself. Her glorious voice had never been more beautiful. At the end of the evening Zygmunt called Theodore to the front of the grand ballroom. He removed a gold chain and pendant from his own neck and placed it around Theo's saying, "Wear this always and keep the promise alive."

Zygmunt died in *Flowers* four cycles later at age forty-five from complications still related to the hornet attack. He had been so happy to celebrate those final Festivals. Bo had snuck his parents back to the beam as often as possible during those cycles to bathe in its warmth and peace, secure in the secret they shared.

## No One Stands at the End of the Rainbow

Every Nobby, young and old, knew the name of Zygmunt. He was the most famous Nobby who had ever lived and his singular size was exceeded only by that of his son, Theodore. News of his death met with great sorrow. Shops and schools closed, and all commerce ceased. Expressions of sympathy flooded into Thistleville. Nobbies everywhere traveled to pay respect. The outpouring was so great, Theo had to convene an emergency session of the Central Council of Elders. Parents brought children so they would see and remember. It was a profound moment in Nobby history, perhaps even a turning point.

The entire ground floor of the Tavern had to be cleared. Zygmunt's body, wrapped first in cloth treated with balm and then clothed in a violet robe trimmed in red, lay on an elevated bed of interwoven boughs gathered from fir trees in the yard. The colors and scent of flowers filled the tavern and spilled out into the village. Four lines stretching around the tavern to the edge of the forest moved in silence as Nobbies came to say goodbye. It took two days for all to pass. Each night, out of respect, every visitor retired to the sanctuary of the forest to provide privacy for the family and the grieving townsfolk of Thistleville.

On the morning of the tenth day of *Flowers*, Zygmunt was carried in honor on the shoulders of the Nobby patrol who had served so well so many cycles earlier. Nobbies lined the pathway from the tavern, around the village square and the outskirts of the village, all the way to a clearing at the edge of the forest. Young drummers tapped a simple, solitary rhythm as the Council of Elders began the solemn procession. Irene, flanked by Bo, Theodore, Astrid, and young Alec, walked in step behind the Nobby patrol. It seemed that every Nobby heart beat in unison with the drums, and all breathed only as the beat gave way to an occasional flourish. A brilliant carpet of flowers covered the path. Profound silence accentuated the crisp steady beat of the drums. The forest, itself, was strangely quiet.

At the simple grave sight, Bo held his mother's hand as he spoke:

"Dear friends, your kind presence here to note the passing of a husband, father, grandfather, and friend, is most appreciated. Sharing such sorrow does somehow make it easier to bear. More important, however, is his memory—who he was, what he did, and what he leaves behind. We each have gifts according to our abilities, gifts to share with each other. My father never failed to answer a call, to extend his hand in service. He taught me a poem awhile back. It has changed my life. I offer it to you today as the expression of his legacy and sacrifice:

*"Intelligence bound by love must always rule,*
*force cannot sustain.*
*One engenders vision and harmony;*
*the other only ignorance and disdain."*

After Zygmunt's death, Irene devoted most of her time compiling a manuscript about the healing properties of fruits, flowers, herbs, and spices. She composed music and played happily with her only grandchild, Alec. It would take another lifetime of new memories to fill the gaping hole in her heart.

Thistleville and all the regions continued to grow and prosper over the next three cycles. The Central Council of Elders worked even better than expected. Theo was the unanimous choice to serve as its first and so far, only Chancellor. When Bo was not removing pests and other dangers as his father had done, he was teaching special skills to young Nobbies or training animals and insects to assist in mining and transportation chores. What he enjoyed most, however, was the tranquil solitude of his new laboratory built in the clearing next to the tavern. It was here that he found happiness, immersed in the thrill of discovery and the wonder of mysteries yet to be unraveled. His most welcome distraction was young Alec, now three.

Alec was a precocious child. He had learned to read at age three, began playing the thistleharp at five, and now was engrossed in science experiments with Uncle Bo at age seven. He also clearly had inherited Theo's leadership charisma and his grandfather Adrian's penchant for organizing things. Although very athletic, his features and temperament were refined as his mother's, and his size was quite ordinary considering the giant muscular frame of his father. There was little doubt that Alec was a marvelous blend of all that symbolized the best in Nobby culture.

Since that ill-fated night of the hornet attack and Zygmunt's aborted mission to the bog, there had been no incidents along the trails. No sightings. No sounds. Whatever it was, if anything, it was gone. No one was complaining. It did raise, however, at least a few theoretical questions about the best way to guard against any future dangers from the outside. Should the Central Council institute a special tax to form and train a Nobby militia? This idea was foreign to Nobby culture. Nobbies always had been peaceful.

What about building a series of outposts? Young Nobbies could be assigned to them in small groups to provide an early warning about intruders. This idea met with great resistance from every Nobby mother. It was far too risky and placed the young in harm's way. It was clear that such a serious question about long-term Nobby security would require further study and debate. This was indeed a proper question for the Central Council to consider and answer.

Because of his unique leadership role, Theo now stood at center stage. He had solved so many other problems before, why not this one? It was ironic that the issue of regional safety generated so much interest at a time when there was actually no threat. Peace and quiet had reigned for so many cycles—there was not even the slightest hint of danger.

## A Kingdom Is Born

Regional growth and security are priorities! Tomorrow is the beginning of *Sun* and Nobbies from Faba, Ogle, Kora and Thistleville have gathered once again to celebrate the Longest Day. Every room is taken. Every vacant space in the town is filled with tents and campfires. Joy, celebration, anticipation, and excitement fill the air. It's a special time, a once in a lifetime event, a moment to be etched forever in the pages of Nobby history.

The Central Council of Elders has scheduled a secret meeting for this evening—a meeting without the Chancellor. Furthermore, plans for a plenary session of the Council involving all regional delegates and visitors are underway for the morning. Chancellor Theodore overhears two elders discussing these plans as he is about to enter the side door of the tavern. Confused, he moves quickly instead to Bo's laboratory.

"Bo, have you been in the village square or gone outside the tavern? Something is going on! The town is crazy! There's dancing and singing everywhere! I've never seen anything like it! What's going on? And the Elders are holding a secret meeting tonight without me! Do you know about this? It's crazy!"

"Theo, what are you raving about? Calm down! You're going so fast, I can't keep up with you!"

"The *meetings*, Bo! What about these *meetings*?"

Bo could only shake his head. He had no idea what Theo was ranting about. He knew nothing about meetings tonight or any other time. He slid back from his bench, and as he walked toward Theo, his mother appeared in the doorway.

"Bo! Theo! What is going on? Nobbies are running all over the place giggling and whispering!"

Irene was right; so was Theo. No doubt about it, something big was going on. Something huge was about to happen; something that would change their lives and alter the course of Nobby history. It was a spontaneous outpouring of love, devotion, appreciation, and trust all rolled into the magic of the moment. It also was no mystery that all *but* the first family of Thistleville should know the secret. After all, this was to be a surprise party. This would be a feast of unprecedented pomp. It was to be the making of a royal family and the coronation of a king. It was nothing less than the birth of a kingdom!

## A Kingdom is Born

The secret meeting of the Council was held that evening with only one item on the agenda—the establishment of a monarchy. The Elders agreed unanimously, but since there never had been a royal family, one had to be named. As Zygmunt's life was recounted from his humble beginnings as an orphan raised in the woods to his heroic deeds to his life of service with Irene to the tragic battle with the hornets and the proud legacy of his two sons, the choice was easy. Zygmunt was the seed of royalty. His family would hold the seat of honor on the throne of the new kingdom. The name of the kingdom? It would be a kingdom named after the village of his birth and the site of his final resting place. It would be the Kingdom of Thistledom.

The Council then turned its attention to the sons. The deeds of both were already legendary. Bo was first. The Elders recognized his unique gifts and powers and, after a long discussion, realized Bo already had a special calling beyond their abilities to understand. However, Theodore was a known treasure, whose administrative and leadership abilities were already tested, steady, and strong—qualities of spirit equal to his tremendous physical size and strength. Theodore would be king, and Astrid his queen, fusing together the four provinces into a single unified land. His vision would become their mission. His ideals would be their goals. His dreams would fashion and form their destiny.

So, it was done. The Council sent a delegation to Irene's home atop the tavern. Out of deference to her own unique role, she would be the first to hear the news. Tears of joy fell softly on Zygmunt's favorite evening robe as she hugged it to her breast. It was a proud moment, a truly magnificent honor. She smiled warmly and thanked the Elders for their gracious gesture. She couldn't help think of the medallion hanging from her son's powerful neck: "A Seed's Power Lies in its Promise." The inscription took on new meaning.

Several Elders depart hastily to visit Theodore's home and Bo's loft. Theodore is drafting a plan for Council review regarding the need for better regional security when the knock came on his door.

"Please come and join the Elders in your mother's chambers."

Bo was smiling and very happy when he opened his door *before* the visitors even had a chance to knock. There was little his dear mother could hide from him.

The evening visit in the upper chambers was brief. As Head of the Council of Elders, Astrid's father, Adrian, spoke for the entire delegation. He disclosed the result of their earlier secret meeting and the coronation plans for the morrow. Theodore was speechless. Amidst all the hugging and excitement, no one noticed the gentle breeze that filled the room, softly fanning the candle flames until they danced with delight.

There was little sleep this night. Preparations, once underway behind the scenes in secret locations, were now full blown in the town square. It was the middle of the night, but looked like midday at Festival time as hundreds of Nobbies worked by moonlight and flaming campfires, building platforms, tables, and booths for the coronation. Spirits soared even higher than the sound of songs in the cool night air.

Thanks to young Nobbies moving up and down trees like squirrels, flags flying the new royal crest of Thistledom suddenly appeared everywhere along with hundreds of blue and yellow banners lined with pink ribbons. The crest was quite striking. It was formed by a circle of thistleleaves placed on a large heart-shaped shield. A smaller outline of the shield filled the center. Inside of it, a great horned owl clutched a snake, and an ancient stringed instrument appeared—all symbols of Nobby past. A thistle stood proudly rooted at the bottom center-point of the thistleleaves; a crown graced the central top point. At the top, in the space between the center shield and the inner circle formed by the leaves, were the words *Pride, Loyalty, Honor, Service.* In the same space at the bottom of the crest on each side of the thistle are the words *The Power of a Seed Lies in its Promise.*

One final note about the royal crest: at the very top was a banner with one word: *Thistledom*. Underneath this was another banner, *the DuBois royal family crest*. By custom Nobbies had never used family names. Nobby historians tell us that this particular name, *DuBois*, was selected to designate the royal family because it means "from the woods," a most fitting name for a royal family rooted in an orphan named Zygmunt.

Wild flowers tinged with every hue of the rainbow filled the square as basket after basket arrived from the surrounding hills. The tavern itself, adorned from top to bottom with banners, flags, and streamers, glowed against the dark mountainside. Even at night, the town square was becoming a feast for the nose, as well as the eyes.

By its very nature, birth is new life, and that's exactly what fired the hearts and minds of those lucky

## A Kingdom is Born

enough to be part of this glorious moment. There is no work in a labor of love. Today, a king would be crowned, and a kingdom born.

The fury of the work pace stopped just before dawn to allow everyone a few winks. After all, the Longest Day was about to begin. Only the Elders moved about town quietly noting and checking each detail. So much accomplished in so short a time was a testimony to the love and respect of the populace for this amazing family. Nothing seemed impossible for the Nobby spirit.

As he had done so often, Bo stepped onto the balcony of his loft in the soft gray light of morning to watch the very first ray of sun dart over the mountain. It was always a glorious moment to stand alone in the silence and wonder. As he stood in awe this morning, humbled by the sight and still stunned by the incredible revelations of the night before, he spotted another solitary figure. It was Theo kneeling in prayer. The brilliance of those first rays struck his bowed head. His golden hair glowed as if he already bore the crown. Bo smiled and stepped back into the shadows. He loved his brother more than anything. Without any doubt, he knew that Theo would be a good and great king. Bo whispered his own private prayer for Theo. "There is much to be done, and not much time," he mused. "Dad would be so proud."

Two hours had barely passed since sunrise, and there was activity all over the village. The aroma of fresh breads, puddings, and strudel eclipsed the wondrous smell of pine wet with dew. Not a cloud in the sky. The town square, the tavern, the streets, and now every house and tent were resplendent with the sun-drenched colors of the DuBois family royal crest. The scene grew even more spectacular as villagers and guests emerged in their finest gowns, britches, and waistcoats. Spirits soared and hearts pounded as the sun rose higher in the morning sky and the magical moment drew closer.

    There was a steady parade of pride to the square all morning. All eyes turned toward the balcony of the tavern. Theodore and Astrid would appear here first, and then come in procession behind the Elders to center stage in the square. Counselor Adrian, ranking Council Elder and father of Astrid, would administer the solemn oath of office to Theodore. All would pledge allegiance to him. Then with a final fanfare, his mother would crown him King Theodore. The doors of the chamber above the tavern opened. Trumpets filled the air. Their echoes rolled across the village in majestic waves magnifying their regal beauty a thousand fold.

    Led by Counselor Adrian, the Elders marched two by two through the main doors of the tavern and moved around to the side garden beneath the balcony. Theodore and Astrid emerged, arm in arm, dressed in stunning red robes trimmed in silver and gold thread. Irene, Bo, and young Alec joined them, and for the first time, cheering subjects of Thistledom saw their Royal Family DuBois. The square could not contain the outpouring of applause and cheers that gushed in torrents from the crowd and rushed down the mountainside to the valleys and bogs below. There was an uneasy rustle in the tall marsh

## A Kingdom is Born

grass, and several reeds quickly parted. The noise of the celebration had not gone unnoticed.

Amid continuous applause, the royal family followed the Elders to the square. The procession split at the center of the platform to form an honor guard. Theodore and Astrid walked through their midst, climbed the steps, and moved to thrones at center stage. When they were seated Irene, Bo, and Alec were escorted to a place of honor. Two goose-down pillows were placed on the floor in front of the thrones. The moment had finally arrived. Astrid's father appeared, bowed reverently to Theodore and Astrid, to the other members of the new royal family, and then turned to address the silent throng. In a deep voice filled with passion and power, he began.

"Fellow citizens! This is the proudest moment of my life as I stand before you to proclaim the coronation of King Theodore and Queen Astrid—the first royal rulers of the Kingdom of Thistledom. It is my privilege to administer the solemn oath of office and to lay the mantle of regal authority across his broad shoulders. Theodore, please rise and bow your head.

"By the will and consent of citizens throughout Thistledom, we name you head of the Royal Family DuBois and charge you with the power and responsibility of governing the sovereign Kingdom of Thistledom. It shall be your solemn duty to protect the realm, preserve the dignity of individual rights, and lead us forward to the future. In return for our solemn pledge of fidelity, and our promise to preserve, protect, and perpetuate the Monarchy of Thistledom and the rights of the Royal Family DuBois, do you, Theodore DuBois, swear by He who created the heavens and earth, who set the beam of the North Star in place, and who guides all things with an inner rhythm and grace; do you swear to accept without reserve the regal rights, responsibilities, and role now offered to you and your descendants as our king?"

The silence was almost too much to bear as Theo turned and gazed at the throng. Every Nobby felt the power, as if the king had looked personally at each of them. Stretching his great arms out as if to embrace them, he responded in a slow measured voice.

"In the name of my mother, Irene, in memory of my father, Zygmunt, in the presence of my brother, Bo, for the love of Astrid and Alec, and with eternal gratitude to you, Counselor Adrian, and for the glory of all the citizens of Thistledom: Yes! I do accept!"

A young attendant holding a dazzling white cloth approached. Counselor Adrian took it carefully and draping it over Theodore's right shoulder said, "Theodore DuBois, receive this seamless mantle of finest lace as a symbol of the authority bestowed upon your person here today, and to your heirs in the tomorrows that will follow. And now, I ask that you and Astrid kneel before your thrones to receive the crowns of the Kingdom of Thistledom."

Irene stood and, with Bo and Alec at her side, slowly approached. Attendants presented two gold

## A Kingdom is Born

crowns laden with jewels. They were exquisite. Her hands trembled as Bo handed her the larger crown. She cradled it in her arms for a moment, then placed it upon her son's head. Bo handed her the second, and she placed it softly on Astrid's bowed head. This was the moment!

The cheers and dancing shattered the silence like an unexpected clap of thunder during a gentle rain. There would be no holding back now! Thistledom had its king and queen. A chorus of cheers rang out in succession. "Long live King Theodore and Queen Astrid! Blessings to the DuBois family! Blessings to Nobbies everywhere! Thistledom forever! Peace to all!"

"Okay, Julia, that's all for now. It's time to rest. The sunlight is peeking through the window. I'll continue later when we have more time. Don't worry! I'll tell you about your father and how you became queen, but for now, you must rest. So many are depending upon your strength."

Julia did not argue. She loved listening to Lord Norbert, but even so, sleep was impossible to resist any longer. It was a short walk to her bedchamber and the soft blissful caress of her pillow. She was indeed a beautiful young queen, a rosebud bursting into full bloom. Good wishes and gifts would fill this special day. She also would know the added wonder of Nobby noesis, the special ability to communicate by thought. It was a marvelous gift, which came mysteriously to all Nobbies at the beginning of their sixteenth cycle. No one knew why or how. But for now, blessed sleep to renew mind and body.

It was nearly ten o'clock when Princess Emily, Julia's older sister, woke her. "C'mon Julia! You can't sleep your birthday away. It's time to party! Wait until you see all the decorations! And the *food*!"

Julia rose quickly, but with a little less vigor than usual. It was an exciting day! She tucked her toes into slippers at her bedside and thought, *Thank goodness Emily has energy enough for both of us.*

Emily immediately laughed and responded, "I sure do! Don't worry, Julia, I plan to take you everywhere today, even if I have to carry you!"

Julia looked at her sister in amazement. It was her first experience with noesis. She would soon learn how to control her thoughts—to share them or keep them to herself. For now, however, it was quite exciting. She wondered how Lord Norbert was, but not for long. He was waiting for her inquiry and his thoughts quickly returned, *I'm fine! Just walking in the orchards outside the castle walls.*

It was a great day. Cousins Stephen and Ellen arrived from Faba in time to join a luncheon celebration planned by Princess Emily. They presented Julia with a beautiful miniature of DuBois Castle made from copper and bronze. The detail was remarkable, even to the shutters at each window and the royal crest etched in the wall over the main gate. All agreed that it would be a wonderful addition to the Royal Art Collection in the throne room.

## A Kingdom is Born

Uncle Richard and Lady Kathy offered a toast to Queen Julia filled with good wishes from all her subjects in the Province of Faba. Nobbies there were celebrating both her birthday and tenth anniversary as queen with a special week-long festival. Following lunch, Princess Emily led the royal party to the courtyard where fifty carriages waited to leave on an afternoon outing. Hundreds of local Nobbies awaited her arrival so the games could begin. A stairway and platform were built high into a tree so Queen Julia could watch the competition and award ribbons to the victors. She was pleasantly surprised when her older cousins, Aaron, Paul, and Meaghan, arrived from Ogle with their parents, Prince John and Lady Catherine. She had not seen them for almost two cycles. It was wonderful to have the family together again.

The afternoon passed quickly and after the last prize was awarded, the members of the royal family returned to the castle. It had been a long, busy day, and Princess Emily had plans for a perfect ending. First, they would gather in the throne room so Julia could open presents. Then, off to the main dining room for birthday puddings and pastries. No one would go to bed hungry this night!

Julia was overwhelmed and a bit embarrassed at the outpouring of attention and so many gifts. She heaved a sigh of relief when Lord Norbert entered the hall and sat beside her. She hadn't seen him all day.

"Good evening! I was worried when I didn't see you earlier today. I thought you might be sick from exhaustion."

"Oh no, Julia, I've never felt better. I had a few things to do and, you know, some celebrations are best left to the young. I figured it safer to join the party after all of you slowed down a bit!"

Julia laughed and squeezed his arm. It was so like him to keep in the background.

As the hours passed, the celebration waned and guests retired to special quarters in the castle. Only Julia, Emily, and their cousins remained with Lord Norbert. It was just like old times. They had spent many hours together with him as young children. Still excited from last evening's revelations about the kingdom, Julia couldn't resist the opportunity to hear more. The setting was perfect. Placing his hand in hers, she asked, "Lord Norbert, a story from you would be a perfect ending to my perfect day. Would you favor us with a story from the past—please?"

Before he could respond, Aaron and Paul were moving chairs. In a flash, they were all seated in front of him—waiting. Lord Norbert raised his hands in a fit of laughter. This scene surely did stir old and pleasant memories. Nodding his head, he responded, "All right! I guess the vote is unanimous! Where should I begin? What is it that you would like to know? There are so many things!"

Julia wasted no time. "Could you tell us about the castle? How it came to be? Who designed it? Who built it and when?"

Young Stephen added, "And what about all those big old beams and the shutters that close over the windows? They look like wood but feel more like rock! What is this material? Who made it?"

Sister Ellen blurted, "Who decided where to build the castle and how long did it take?"

Emily tried to make it simple. "Lord Norbert, tell everything you know. Every single detail! We don't care how long it takes!"

These were all good questions, and there were many more besides. Lord Norbert knew he was no longer dealing with a short story. It would take some time, and some background, for them to understand everything. He thought, *Is this the right time? It will not be easy for them. Should they know? Knowledge can be painful. Do they have a right to know? Yes! After all, it is their legacy.*

As was his custom, Lord Norbert closed his eyes for a moment to gather his thoughts. Everyone moved frantically to be ready when they opened. It seemed like forever before he began.

# The Mystery of the Bog

"Before Thistledom, and long before this castle, Nobbies lived in four regions spread across the Land of the Mitten. You know the names well: Faba, Kora, Ogle, and Thistleville. Life in these regions remained the same for generations until the appearance of one of our greatest heroes of the past, a Nobby named Zygmunt, born in the tiny hamlet of Thistleville. He was a giant in stature as well as heart, standing a full thistle leaf taller than any other Nobby of the time. His deeds of bravery became legendary, especially his courageous battle with a swarm of hornets which ultimately would cost him his life."

"What happened?" Paul asked. "Can you tell us about the hornets?"

Lord Norbert smiled and responded, "Ask Julia. She can tell you the whole story later."

He continued, "Zygmunt married Irene, a beautiful, dark-haired Nobbess from Kora. Her legacy of songs and writings about healing herbs remain with us to this day."

Suddenly, Lord Norbert's voice faltered, forcing him to pause. He tried to speak, but the words seemed to catch in his throat. Eyes glistening for a moment, he swallowed hard, cleared his throat, and after a very deep breath continued.

"Irene bore two sons. The eldest, known as Bo, favored his mother in talent and temperament. His ingenuity and knowledge about forest life were known throughout the kingdom. His inventions were a big help in the design and construction of this castle. Theodore was born two full cycles after Bo. He was a mirror image of his father and grew even taller. With a quick temper, strong leadership skills, and a flair for bringing order to chaos, he organized the four regions into the kingdom we know today as Thistledom. By acclamation, he became its first ruler. It was at the very beginning of his reign when the idea of a castle first arose. As so often happens, it was an idea born of necessity."

"What do you mean, Lord Norbert?" Emily asked. "Do you mean we were forced to build this huge castle?"

"For a long time, Nobbies had been concerned about strange sounds coming from the bog. Travelers passing near these swamp lands often sensed an eerie presence. So did the animals. And apparently, not every

Nobby passed safely. It was very sad and most disturbing. Even King Theodore's own grandparents had vanished without a trace while traveling this way, leaving his father, Zygmunt, an orphan at age four. As the seasons and cycles passed, this strange presence also would mysteriously come and go. So would those horrible tales of Nobby disappearances and the harrowing fruitless searches. No one knew the dark force hidden within the bog—that is no one alive enough to tell.

"Security was the most important issue as Theodore became king. Nobbies wanted answers. The mystery of the bog had to be solved. King Theodore knew the dangers involved, so he made a choice, a choice not surprising to a single soul. He would personally lead a troop of Nobbies specially chosen to investigate the bog and put this puzzle to rest. If the danger could not be removed peacefully, then he and the Council of Elders would take whatever action required to assure the safety and security of the citizens of Thistledom. The decision was made, now a plan had to be devised—but a plan that would be safer than the one that had so damaged and shortened his father's life.

"A measure of King Theodore's greatness was the awareness of his own limitations. Remembering the plan his brother had devised to get rid of hornets many cycles earlier, his first decision was easy. He knew well the profound difference between thinking and doing, planning and execution, design and implementation. These are two separate and very different talents. While both are necessary, most often, they are not found together.

# The Mystery of the Bog

King Theodore knew this. Since Bo had once devised a successful plan, why not again? They always had been a strong team. If Bo would plan it, he would do it!

"For the next several days and nights, the brothers spent every minute planning, challenging, re-planning, and rethinking. Whatever they would do, it must be foolproof. While danger and the unknown were unwanted elements they could accept; surprise and error were not. The plan must provide maximum information about the bog, but minimal exposure to it and whatever secrets it held. Finally, they had a plan."

It was the time of *Colors*, and soon the leaves would fall. They must move soon to take full advantage of the cover provided by the dense foliage in and around the bog. King Theodore and Bo asked for volunteers. The ten members of the old Nobby patrol were the first to step forward. They would not be denied. So, the team was set. It was now time for the plan. A meeting took place in Bo's laboratory.

King Theodore began, "Thanks for being here and for your willingness to once again place yourselves in harm's way. Bo will give you the details."

"As you well remember, when our father tried to solve the mystery of the bog, he met with disaster. He never even got there. He learned nothing and lost everything. To eliminate similar dangers and to multiply our chances of simultaneously surveying large sections of the bog during a single mission, I am training great horned owls to carry us under cover of night. For some time now, I have studied the swamp from afar in the tallest firs at the edge of the tree line. Though the swamp is a very large area, I've plotted a grid using trees in the bog as reference points. Each of us is assigned a number of these trees. It will be much easier to divide and study this massive area.

"Tomorrow night we will fly the owls to the first set of trees. Once we land, we must hide and rest at the top of the trees. As they would normally do, the owls will hunt in the swamp, but stay close enough to protect us while we sleep. During the next day, stay in the trees and observe as much as you can in every direction. Take note of anything unusual or any unfamiliar sounds. The owls will hide by day, but return at nightfall to pick us up. Go to the second set of trees and repeat the assignment. We will not be able to see each other all the time. Stay in touch, but make no noise! We are there to see, not to be seen! It will take four days and nights to cover just the closest end of the bog. At dawn on the fifth morning, we will return to Thistleville. Travel light. Take a double reed hammock so you cannot fall if the wind blows hard. Eat only cold snacks. No fires! If someone or something is there, we'll see it! And by the way, don't worry! The owls already know the trees assigned to each of you. Trust them. They will not fail you."

The following evening came quickly. The days were getting shorter at this time in the cycle. It was difficult to separate excitement from the tension felt in the village. All of the members of the former Nobby patrol were married now except Bo. Some had small children. There was no doubt about the bravery or confidence of the patrol—it was high. The forced smiles of wives and mothers, however, betrayed a much stronger sentiment. King Theodore saw it in Astrid's eyes as well. He recognized their fear and spoke directly to it.

"I know you are worried. But I assure you that no one will be harmed on this mission. I promise! We will stay hidden and collect only information. Bo's plan is excellent and devised with safety as the priority. In the quiet of evening, you will know how we are doing. For the sake of us all, we must do this. Think only good thoughts and remember that knowledge is power. That alone is what we seek at this time. I promise we will *all* return promptly and safely."

The power and sincerity in Theodore's voice provided the perfect medicine. Everyone felt better. He had spoken and they believed. After all, was he not King Theodore, the most powerful force in all of Thistledom? With light hearts, the excursion party took leave of family members and moved to the center of the clearing north of the tavern. Hammocks, snacks, and camouflage clothing were all tightly packed and slung over their shoulders. Bo moved to the edge of the forest while Theodore gave a final reassurance to Queen Astrid and to his mother. As he reached to jostle young Alec's hair, the owls began to glide silently into the clearing. It was time to go. King Theodore turned away, looked at the sky, and took one very deep breath. Yes, he was king, but had no super powers. He was worried, but there was little moonlight. That was a plus!

It was a rare and magnificent sight to see even one great horned owl, yet there they were, a dozen perched on a fallen tree just inside the far end of the clearing, and standing as still as stones. The sight was so unusual, even the children were dumbstruck. All watched intently. It surely was a sight to remember and describe for generations.

Bo moved quickly. Owls do not like the open. As he approached, each one lowered its head to receive a short loop of rope. Standing before the last owl he whistled softly and all leaned forward. Bo motioned for the patrol to approach. They did and carefully climbed aboard. No one had ever done this before. Straddling the owls' powerful necks, they grabbed hold of the ropes and waited silently for Bo.

King Theodore was the last to mount. His was the largest owl anyone had ever seen. When he was ready, Bo whistled and the owls took flight. Their enormous outstretched wings became a blur in pale moonlight visible only momentarily through parting clouds. Fluttering rapidly, powerful wing muscles snapped the air like whips as the great birds strained to leave the ground. Despite the weight, they rose swiftly above the center of the clearing. Once in the air, their wings spread wide as they soared silently overhead. Then within the blink of an eye, they were gone.

Irene joined many wives and mothers that night in silent prayer. The awful waiting had begun. Very much alone, her tears fell softly on Zygmunt's robe until sleep finally dried her eyes and drained her mind of worry.

The flight to the bog was spectacular, revealing a breathtaking landscape of shadows and light. Bo marveled how the owl saw the slightest movement on the ground from this height and in so many shadows. They were solitary creatures. It was a special thrill to see them fly together carrying the patrol. He was pleased. King Theodore noticed that the swamp below held a special irony. It seemed to reflect more light at night than during the day, and certainly had more sounds. From this view high overhead, the kingdom was very peaceful.

The steep, silent glide from the heavens to the treetops was exhilarating. Maneuvering with but a few feathers, the owls landed effortlessly in their assigned trees. So far, so good! It was time to settle in, secure supplies, and rest. There was no doubt, however, that the loudest noises in the bog were the heartbeats of these visiting Nobby sentinels. Rest was possible, but there would be precious little sleep.

The period just before dawn is unique. There is a total silence. Night creatures have gone to rest and those of the day have not yet risen. Even the winds cease. For these few brief moments, time itself seems to stand still, pausing for its own rest. Alone at his post overlooking the central portion of the swamp, King Theodore observed the silence and couldn't help wonder what it was hiding.

What would they find?

That first day came and went without incident. Nothing happened. Only familiar creatures like birds, turtles, and snakes moved above, on, and in the swamp. There were no unusual noises, no unexpected events, no unexplained behaviors. The bog was a tranquil world unto itself. Just after dusk, the owls reappeared. Within a few moments, each Nobby was taken to a new perch deeper into the swamp. It was comforting to remember Bo's earlier words, "Don't worry! The owls know the trees. Trust them. They will not fail you."

Dawn on the second day brought more of the same. There was surely a natural order in the swamp that included struggle and death, as well as life. But the violence was always brief and without malice. There was purpose and order, a natural law that was constant and supreme. The only noticeable change at this new location was the size of the island-forming reeds and swamp grass. These islands were a bit higher and wider. Noetic conversation that evening helped all rest better, those alone at home, as well as those alone in the swamp.

It was obvious very early that the third day would not be pleasant. The sky filled with ominous clouds. Wind gusts pushed the trees as if they were wispy reeds. Shallow water churned by the weeds and grass frothed so the entire swamp seemed transformed into a monster, foaming at the mouth, about to devour everything in its grasp. It was all they could do to hang onto the tree limbs to escape the rampaging creature below. Food was lost, some hammocks blown away, but all survived the onslaught. Nightfall brought peace. There was no moon. The price of friendly clouds covering them in a protective blanket was total darkness—a darkness that tested even the keenest Nobby eyes. There was no worry, however, because the owls returned once again. The trip this night deeper into the swamp would be the final leg in the journey. Whether from the darkness or the exhaustion from the battles of the day, they spent little time settling in for the night. They tied themselves securely to limbs and slept. The owls would have to pay special attention tonight.

What a difference a day makes! Dawn was breathtaking. Every sight and sound seemed magnified in the crisp morning air. As the sun rose higher, Theodore noticed shadowy clumps under some of the larger trees on an adjacent island. They looked like random mounds of swamp grass blown into piles by the storm. It wasn't until after midday that the sunlight revealed even more mounds—and the holes in them. Upon closer scrutiny, they were not just piles of debris blown together by wind and water, they were huts! What a discovery! But who built them? How? Where were they now? The swamp appeared deserted. No signs of life. No fires. No movement. No sounds.

Theodore needed more information. He had promised that the patrol would remain hidden. And so it would. He summoned Bo from the far end of the bog. A monstrous red-tail hawk provided passage. They talked for some time. Theodore wanted to take a closer look at the huts.

Bo cautioned against it saying, "Remember! No surprises and no errors!"

Theodore insisted, "We're too close! Who lives here? We must know! Now is the time! It may be our only chance to find out."

Bo knew it was useless to resist. He alerted the others to remain hidden and to return to Thistleville in the morning as planned—without them, if necessary. "This was the command of the king!"

He slid down to the base of the tree. Before Theodore had time to join him, a large snapping turtle raised its head through the green slime near his feet. Bo smiled. When Theodore reached the ground, both grabbed handfuls of reeds and grass. Stepping carefully onto the turtle's back, they dropped to one knee and covered themselves with the foliage. The turtle edged lazily away from the bank. Two members of the patrol watched realizing that as the brothers disappeared into the marsh, all of Thistledom was in peril. Local noetic chatter filled the air with but one message, "No way will we ever leave the bog without King Theodore and Bo. Not a chance!"

Theodore was the first to jump to shore. Together they crawled through the wet weeds and then the shorter grass, right up to the large opening in the closest hut. The scene and circumstance reminded them of another time and place, one involving a large hornet nest. They waited for a long time, watching and listening. There

## The Mystery of the Bog

was no one around. Finally, Theodore stood and walked boldly through the opening in the hut, disappearing into the dark inner core.

Bo waited. There was no noise inside the hut. That was good! Lying on his stomach, he waited and watched, eyes locked on the entrance and straining to see into the shadows. He was concentrating so hard, the snake was at his feet before he sensed it. With tongue darting as fast as an eyelash, it paused, uncertain about its discovery. Was it food? Bo rolled quickly to the side and jumped to his feet. They were eye to eye. Heart still pounding, he slowly stretched out his hand. The snake's black shiny eyes focused on the hand and followed every movement.

Bo had never before been this close to so large a snake. Its head was massive, larger than his own. And the eyes, a chilling, unwavering black stare incapable of feeling. Its tongue moved even faster now, like a razor slicing the air into minute invisible particles of taste and smell. The uneasy standoff lasted only a few seconds. Green eyes against black. Then suddenly and without hesitation, Bo tapped it smartly on the nose with the palm of his hand. This was *not* food! The snake lowered its head and slithered away scarcely moving a single reed. Bo watched. It was a very *long* snake. As he turned back toward the hut, Theodore emerged struggling with two large items. Bo rushed to meet him, and together they hauled the things into the reeds for cover.

"What are these?" Bo asked.

"I'm not sure! The one seems to be a huge shoe, or sandal. Imagine that! From heel to toe, it stretches as high as my waist! The other looks like a strap or belt. Feel the sharp stones glued to it! There were also tall three-legged stools and big tables inside. And the most awful smelling clothes! Foul giants must live here!"

Theodore was strong, but what would his strength mean against such size? Bo reacted instinctively. There were lots of huts, and large fire pits scattered about. No way of telling when the inhabitants would return, and they were a long way from the safety of the trees. He motioned to Theodore, "Let's go!"

Theodore dropped the large shoe there in the reeds. He coiled the studded strap though, and placed it over his head and shoulder. Bo led the way back through the reeds to the water. As if on cue, the great turtle raised its head and glided closer to pick them up. It felt good to leave the huts. They were indeed a very long way from the safety of Thistleville. Seeing the huts and just thinking about the size of those who lived there, they had good reason now to question even the safety of Thistledom itself. They agreed to keep this new and disturbing information between them until they could learn more. At least now, they knew where to look. The *what* and the *who*, however, still remained a mystery. As the turtle glided to a stop and climbed the mucky bank on the opposite shore, they looked back across the open swamp. Both knew they would return.

The trip home in the pre-dawn darkness was quick and quiet. As the first rays of light appeared, the owls slid silently into the clearing by the tavern on currents of cool morning air. The grace of their movement was something to see, blurred feathers of light flashing against the dark background of the forest. Everyone was safe. Irene watched alone from her balcony. Bo waved. She would rest easy now. The patrol huddled briefly under her window before departing to their homes and their waiting families.

Two days later King Theodore summoned the Council of Elders to describe the size of the swamp and to report the fact that the patrol had not seen anyone. He recommended a second trip in a fortnight to explore more remote areas. As a precaution, he forbade any further travel along Binder's Trail. Word of the ban spread throughout the kingdom and even though the mystery of the bog remained, Nobbies everywhere took great solace in the personal protection of their king.

King Theodore hid his true feelings well. Neither Queen Astrid nor his mother knew the deep concern he shared with Bo. So, under the guise of another preliminary mapping trip to survey new areas of the swamp in preparation for the next excursion, King Theodore and Bo departed right away the next morning. As far as anyone knew, their plan was to view the farthest areas of the bog from several different vantage points along the tree line. This particular task was safe, but would take time—perhaps as much as two days. Theodore and Bo promised to stay in touch. Queen Astrid and Irene gave them little choice. Neither was pleased.

They would indeed survey the swamp from different vantage points, but only the first would involve the relative safety of the tree line just above the bog. They were on the way back to the huts.

Theodore and Bo followed Binder's Trail straight to the edge of the bog. Fortunately, a cloudless sky provided unusual clarity on the horizon. From their hideaway in a tall maple, they could see easily the areas of the marsh explored earlier. Although individual huts were not visible, they could see the large island mass of moss and weeds that held them. Tonight, they would learn more.

At dusk, two owls made a single pass over the bog, turned sharply and flew directly to Bo's side in the tree. King Theodore recognized the larger one. What a magnificent hunter! Its wingspan stretched nearly ten times as wide as Bo was tall. With dark brown plumage except for a crest of snow-white feathers framed in yellow on its breast, the great horned owl looked more like a ghostly specter in the dim light than a bird. King Theodore imagined the magnificent bird soaring high above the marsh in the black expanse of a moonless night and yet, nothing escaped its stare. Nor if chosen as prey, could anything elude those powerful, deadly talons.

Bo placed a rope collar once again over the bowed head of each bird. It was time to go. Wings fluttering at first, they dropped precipitously from the treetops into the night air. A few powerful strokes later, they rose high above the marsh. Nobby eyes had never before seen such

## The Mystery of the Bog

beauty and majesty. Bathed in moonlight and reflecting the twinkling of countless stars, the marsh below sparkled like a field of fireflies—a tapestry of light, shadow, and texture of such detail and magnitude, one could only imagine the awesome majesty and power of the weaver. In the thrill of the moment, the hidden danger below was forgotten. They had no worries seated atop the owls in flight tonight. No worries, whatsoever.

Bo guided the owls to a lone willow standing at the edge of the island between the open marsh to the north and the huts seen a few nights earlier. They arrived without a sound. No one was there. No activity. The moon was bright and dawn a long way off. After carefully observing the swamp in every direction, both slid down the trunk and dropped softly into tufts of marsh grass on the ground below. They were alone with no time to waste.

As they emerged from the shadow of the willow, the moon slipped briefly behind one lone cloud. Time was now an ally and there would be much to see tonight. Theodore crouched low, waved for Bo to follow, and began to run. Passing large fire pits and perhaps as many as forty huts built along the pathway in a zigzag pattern, they ran all the way to the western most tip of the island. Bo chuckled to himself. They still had it! They could run with the best!

One hut stood alone at the edge of a sandbar jutting out from the main island. It was a large hut strategically placed with an expansive view of the marsh—impossible to approach undetected. It had its own fire pit. Instinctively, they knew this hut was special. Without hesitation, they crossed the open area. The main doorway at the far side facing the open water was at least two stems high. Theodore entered first.

It took a few seconds for their eyes to adjust to the total darkness inside.

"You're right, Theo, giants do live here!"

It was a huge room with a log table and six three-legged stools standing on one side. Another smaller table was pushed against the back wall with several large sacks tucked underneath. The floor of the hut was dirt, packed very hard. A crudely built ladder leaned against the wall opposite the log table. It extended up through a gaping hole in the ceiling. Theo headed for the ladder. Bo returned to the front entrance to be sure they were still alone. By the time he returned, Theo had already scaled the ladder and was rummaging through the upper level. Two boots dropped through the opening, falling with a big thud to the dirt floor. They were huge and heavy, with sharp rough stones glued to the heels and toes. A gigantic hat was the next item to sail through the opening followed by another of those strange studded straps. As Bo picked it up, Theo slid down the ladder. "There isn't much else up there, just several woven cots and some animal skins."

Bo walked to the sacks under the table. They were large. He tugged at the nearest, but it didn't move. Theo added his muscle and over it went, spilling out an odd

## The Mystery of the Bog

assortment of things: broken pieces of pots and chipped dishes, rough pointed stones wrapped in pieces of cloth, leather straps, what looked like broken tools, two old drinking gourds, and some chestnuts.

The second sack contained old boots and sandals, a belt about a leaf and a half wide, several pieces of hard wood that looked like handles of some sort, and a turtle shell. The handles were interesting. They looked like wood but felt like stone. They were heavy too. Bo took a small piece broken off from one of the handles tucking it into his belt.

The last sack was much lighter and startled them as it toppled over by itself. Mostly clothes fell out and several Nobby shoes. They were stunned! Their worst fears had come true. Bo gathered the shoes and headed for the door. A sick feeling gripped his heart. Theodore made one final pass around the room and followed. It was at this moment he vowed that as king, he would not let such a tragedy happen again. It was his responsibility to provide security and he would do just that, no matter what the cost. He was angry! But for the first time in his life, anger gave way to common sense. He was not thinking about getting even or settling a score. He was weighing alternatives, looking at options, considering ways to eliminate or prevent future problems. There was no time for any self-indulging, intoxicating rush of anger. He was thinking and acting like a king.

The marsh was alive. A multitude of creatures croaked, splashed, whined, and droned, creating a lyrical strain that seemed to ebb and flow with the wind and water. Bo and Theo paused briefly in the cover of some tall reeds. There were no unnatural or unusual sounds. They were still alone. Moving steadily back toward the willow, they couldn't resist entering more huts. The findings, however, were the same: tables and stools, cots, a few articles of clothing, and lamps that burned pine tar. All the huts had something else in common. There was no food. Whoever these giants were, one thing was certain—they carried food and most of their possessions with them. A second conclusion was also becoming clear—they planned to return.

Random visits to another half dozen huts turned up nothing new. The dank, musty smell of rotting grass, however, was growing stronger and more oppressive at each turn. They were at high risk being so close to an enemy they didn't even know. Bo's uneasiness increased, and they were only halfway back to the willow. Theo sensed his concern and suggested they split up and do just a quick check of the remaining huts to save time. It was important to learn as much as possible. Lost opportunities rarely return. They would meet back at the willow. Bo agreed, but insisted they not enter the huts, just peer into the entrances.

"Fine!" agreed Theo.

They split. Theo moved to the crooked row nearest the marsh. Bo would take those hugging the main path.

# The Mystery of the Bog

Bo moved quickly inspecting the last ten huts. He reached the willow tree before Theo. Looking out along the edge of the marsh, he saw that Theo had covered only half the distance. Bo watched intently as his brother disappeared around the back of one of the larger huts. Bo waited. He looked out over the southern stretch of the marsh in response to a strange sound, or so he thought. He saw nothing, but still was sure he had heard something. He looked anxiously again for Theo who still hadn't come into view. His thoughts went out, but Theo did not respond. Bo waited. He heard the strange sound again, only louder, and there was more than one sound! He glanced nervously toward the edge of the swamp. Still no Theo! Bo couldn't wait any longer. He moved from the shadows under the tree toward Theo. He had taken only a few strides when Theo reappeared. It was the same instant that he saw a large raft slip ashore behind Theo from the open waters to the north. Bo was upset! An echo had tricked him.

There was no time now! Theo turned, saw the raft, and dropped to the ground. He crawled diagonally away from the huts toward taller reeds at the very edge of the swamp. Bo saw him and did the same. A band of giant trolls got off the raft and stomped right between them to the huts. Other rafts followed close behind, landing all around them. The trolls passed close enough to touch. Some were over two stems tall, others topped three stems. Fortunately, they couldn't see in the dark. Bo rolled twice to keep from getting trampled. Other animals followed the trolls. They were strange three-legged beasts ranging from ten to twenty leafs at the shoulders, with menacing yellow eyes that glowed in the dark. They had two short legs in front, and only one big leg in the back. Growling and snarling, they tugged and bit at each other all the way to the huts.

In no time at all the fire pits roared and foul smelling smoke filled the night air. The females began to tie small chunks of meat to large wooden stakes and stood them in tripod fashion over the fire pits. From his vantage point, Bo recognized the meat as the carcasses of rabbits, swamp rats, and even an occasional snake. He also saw large baskets of apples, corn, and other fruits and vegetables. Because it was the time of *Colors*, he assumed that the trolls were settling in with provisions for the *Shiver* season. This indeed was a sizeable village and well organized. Momentarily distracted by all the activity, Bo's attention returned to Theo. As his eyes searched the darkness along the shoreline, he saw Theo crouched behind a dead tree that had fallen partially into the marsh. Safe for the moment, they would have to wait until the trolls went to sleep before risking their return to the willow.

As Bo watched the action unfold, several trolls walked angrily from their huts to one of the center fire pits. Waving arms wildly, they started looking around the huts and searching along the path. They had realized that something had disturbed their huts. Others grabbed clubs and moved angrily toward the shore where he and Theo were hiding. Many of those three-legged nasties were also turned loose.

Theo saw them coming and remained perfectly still, securely tucked into the shadowy crotch of the fallen tree. It probably saved his life because the snake didn't sense his presence either. Theo had been watching the trolls so intently, he paid no attention to the subtle movement in the reeds to his right. When he did, it was too late. He was trapped, face to face with either capture or certain death. The forked tongue flicked excitedly as the snake picked up his scent. Its huge head drew steadily closer. Cold black eyes stared intently at the warmth detected in the shadow of the log. This prey was trapped! The snake knew it, and so did Theo; and neither cared about the approaching trolls. The snake raised its head high in the grass and coiled back. With fangs gleaming, it rocked backward to strike. How long is a heartbeat?

Angry trolls, several three-legged pets, and Theo all jumped as an eerie shadow swooped silently from the sky and ripped its talons into a very large snake at the shoreline by a fallen tree. It had barely missed their heads! Now airborne, the huge snake writhed and twisted in the moonlight, crippled by its own weight swaying heavy and helpless in the air. The sound of powerful wings snapped loudly in the chilled silence as the giant horned owl rose above the open marsh. The startled trolls first crouched in fear, then cheered wildly, believing the intruder they sought had just received a proper punishment. Still unnoticed, Theo slid slowly back into the shadows, sighed heavily, and whispered thanks to his big brother.

As the night grew colder, the three-legged pets began to howl, high pitched, horrible sounding wails that hurt the ears. When they howled, the marsh became silent. All creatures hid. Eventually, they tired, and when the camp was filled with snores, Bo and Theo returned to safety at the top of the willow.

"Theo! Why did you disappear behind the large hut? You were gone a long time! What happened?"

"You won't believe it, Bo! I found one of our Nobby carriages leaning against the back wall. A wheel was broken and several sideboards were damaged."

"Do you think the trolls did it?"

"I don't know, Bo. It sure looks like it!"

"The camp is peaceful now. We had better get some rest too, Theo. Who knows what will happen tomorrow!"

An unusual bank of warm air engulfed the swamp at dawn. Fog rose from the wet ground like smoke from a thousand fire pits. It was daylight but there wasn't much to see. Bo and Theo worked quietly tying small limbs closer together to provide better cover. They would stay in the tree. It was a good hideout with a great view. They shared a cold snack and watched, waiting for the opening act on the stage below.

The three-legged animals were the first to awake. They appeared clumsy, lurching, and jumping about, but they actually were very powerful and sure-footed. Bo whispered to Theo about a story found long ago on some old scrap of parchment. The creatures described matched this band of trolls and their pets. If they were indeed the same, then these giant trolls were known as Troggs, and their ugly three-legged pets were doogles.

About mid-morning as the haze began to lift, Bo and Theo had their first chance to get a close up look at the Trogg village. Atop the willow, they could see the whole island. Troggs emerged from huts to tend fire pits and feed doogles. There were many more huts than first realized. This was a large village. To think that all this time, it remained hidden in the bog. No wonder Nobbies heard strange sounds. Had the Troggs lived closer to the mainland, undoubtedly they would have been discovered long ago. Theo thought about the broken carriage and the shoes, *If only...*

The day passed quickly. There was activity all over the village, and it was obvious from their dress and aggressive behavior that Troggs were not friendly neighbors. Even the young wore those heavy black boots with rough stones glued to the heels and toes. The largest Troggs stood nearly three stems tall and weighed at least five times more than King Theodore, himself, who was by far the biggest Nobby in the land standing at eight lfs and weighing thirty-two kbgs. Broad leathery straps crisscrossed their chests and were hooked to a wider waist belt. Everything was studded with stones. Male Troggs wore tight britches, and the females wore long pants with very baggy legs. Many Troggs had large, wide-brimmed hats woven from reeds and grass. Some of the younger females tied a three-cornered cloth at the forehead. Still others wore a single leather strap wrapped tightly around the forehead to hold back long hair.

Young Troggs spent the day wrestling, fighting with doogles, beating clubs against trees and shrubs, and chasing an occasional snake or turtle. Adults cut reeds, repaired huts, cleared fire pits, and tended the very young. They also carried sacks from many of the rafts filled apparently with more booty. Trogg behavior was very rough by Nobby standards, and so was their physical appearance.

Most notable was their wrinkly, ashen-gray skin and long matted hair. Adult males had thick patches of hair all over their bodies. Nearly every Trogg had warts. They were much different than Nobbies. Beady, round, reddish eyes, big pointed ears, and short, fat fingers with claw-like nails were commonplace. Most also had yellow crooked teeth, and probably very bad breath from chewing acorns and tree roots and drinking swamp water. Troggs didn't act too friendly, and they certainly didn't look friendly either.

It was early evening when a group of youngsters decided to play under the willow. It seemed like a crazy game, but they had a lot of fun. One Trogg was selected to hurl a large club high into the willow while the others lay spread out on the ground underneath the branches. The club was heavy, and after bouncing from limb to limb, it would fall back to the ground. If it landed on one of the Troggs, the others would all laugh. The game continued for some time and several got hit pretty hard. But the more it hurt, the louder everyone laughed and carried on. It was especially funny when the doogles wandered under the tree and got whacked. It was funny and scary at the same time.

Bo and Theo got a real good look at doogles—very heavy dog-like creatures with big, thick necks. They were covered with dirty, tangled red hair and have green teeth. They really stunk too, like a dirty wet diaper. When they'd get hit, their heads would roll back and necks would stretch way up in the air. The howls that followed were just horrible. With mouths and eyes wide open, Theo and Bo could see their long, slimy blue tongues even in the dimming light. They looked even more fearsome with those big collars spiked with sharp stones.

Unfortunately, the innocent game lasted a bit too long because the club accidentally struck Bo's knapsack knocking it to the ground. The club fell, hitting one Trogg, and the knapsack hit another. Bo and Theo held their breath as it lay unnoticed at the base of the tree. Then the worst happened. The young Trogg who had been hit saw it as he knelt back down and screamed with excitement and surprise. He rushed to show the others, spilling out some food and the Nobby shoes taken from the hut. All eyes turned to the willow, dissecting it branch by branch. Bo and Theo leaned close-in against the limbs, hoping the leaves would provide enough cover. They didn't! The young Troggs pointed straight at them. Startled by something never seen before, they all ran screaming for help.

It would be their only chance. Bo and Theo dropped from limb to limb almost in a straight line and hit the ground running. They took nothing with them. The safest place would be the fallen tree at the edge of the marsh. It was the race of their lives. Luckily, dusk was now giving way to darkness. It would help buy a little time for Bo to work his magic.

The whole Trogg village returned and surrounded the willow. Everyone was pointing to the top and throwing clubs. A few carried pine-tar torches and started climbing the tree. The rocking hammock coupled with their fear of the unknown delayed a final assault to the top branches just long enough to provide a safe retreat.

Bo and Theo dove headlong over the old tree to the safety of its shadow. It was an ugly scene back at the willow. As they watched the pandemonium, Bo leaned heavily against the tree. It felt strange to his touch. He removed the small wooden handle piece from his belt. They were the same. Looked like wood, was wood, but felt like stone. It was puzzling.

The Troggs didn't notice the old turtle surface near the fallen tree. No one saw Bo and Theo lying flat on its back as it swam lazily around the far western tip of the island toward the mainland and freedom.

The din on Trogg Island echoed across the open waters of the marsh for a long time, but by the time the frantic search of the willow widened, Bo and Theo were safe on the distant shore. A close call, to be sure! However,

## The Mystery of the Bog

the mystery was solved. The next step was to solve the problem created by its solution. Within a few minutes, two familiar friends passed silently once overhead, and then glided gracefully to Bo's side at the water's edge.

The flight home was quick and required just a bit more attention because they had no ropes to hold. Balance, however, was not a problem. The owls flew steady and straight. They landed easily in the clearing by the tavern and then disappeared into the forest—unaware of the true significance of their service to the Nobbies of Thistledom. Thankfully, neither Astrid nor Irene saw the mud-caked duo return. There would have been a lot of explaining. They bathed and changed at Bo's place, ate a little, and slept on solid ground. It was good.

The royal family reunited at breakfast. Irene and Queen Astrid were the first to learn about the Troggs. They were relieved the mystery was solved, but worried now about what the future would hold. King Theodore called a meeting of the Elders for the afternoon.

The tavern below was packed even as King Theodore and Bo held a private meeting with the Elders upstairs. Everyone wanted to hear the news. By evening, every Nobby knew about the bog, Troggs, doogles, and the King's command to stay clear of the pathways nearest the bog. A special meeting of the Elders was set for five days hence to consider alternatives, review options, and establish a plan. In the meantime, they were safe. The Troggs did not know who they were, nor where to find them. But for how long?

## DuBois Castle—The Vision

Even with all that he had seen on Trogg Island, it was the handle-like piece of wood that most intrigued Bo. He had never seen any material like it. *Had it come from that old sunken tree at the edge of the island? No matter! What is it? Why is it so hard?*

Bo went to work in his lab learning quickly that the heavy, rock-like wood would not bend or burn. It also was impossible to break. These were very desirable properties. "If that giant old tree were truly the same…" He began to experiment.

Meanwhile, King Theodore worked on his own private plan for security. Aware of the size, strength, and number of the Troggs, he knew the key to Nobby safety was to remain hidden. Nobbies were not warriors, they were farmers and miners. Direct confrontation was out of the question. With the work of several days now behind, he had a three-pronged approach.

## DuBois Castle—The Vision

The Council of Elders was most anxious to hear King Theodore's plan. News about Trogg Island and the giant trolls had at first stirred great excitement, but that moment was over! The stark reality of such a foe so close now caused panic. Parents kept children inside. Regional travel slowed to a trickle. Far too much time and energy were wasted worrying. For Nobbies, to live in the shadows of "What if…" was not good. The Council knew this. Only King Theodore, however, had the power to calm the kingdom, redirect their energy, and tap the awesome potential they possessed. A general meeting of all regional and local leaders was scheduled in a fortnight.

Not a delegate was missing as King Theodore spoke in clear and confident tones to all the assembled leaders of Thistledom.

"Members of the Council of Elders, Regional and Local Delegates:

"Thank you for your kind attendance at this most important meeting. We are at a pivotal point in our history. Serious challenges face us and must be addressed. Our very survival could be at stake! It is a time for us to join hearts and hands, bodies and spirits, friends and neighbors to form a bond the likes of which has never been seen before.

"You are all aware of the potential enemy that lurks in the bogs at the base of the mountain. You have shared agonizing hours searching for lost friends or relatives. No longer can we live with uncertainty and in constant fear. We are born free and by all that we hold sacred, we must maintain our freedom. I've asked you to come because I have a plan to share; a plan that will regain control of our lives, safeguard our travel, and most importantly, prepare us for the future. But if this plan remains solely my plan, it will be of little value. It must become our plan. Please listen.

"First and foremost, we must remain non-violent and peaceful. This is our history: to live in harmony with nature. Troggs do not change this credo by their crude behavior, but their presence clearly changes Nobby life. At all costs then, we will avoid direct contact with Troggs or any others who might threaten our security and peace. The best way to insure this security is to continue our policy of isolation.

"Secondly, I propose to establish a new surveillance system providing constant vigilance over our land, main travel routes, and borders. Accordingly, I hereby establish the Royal Guard of Thistledom, and appoint my close friends, John and James, as Captains of the Guard. They are charged with the task of implementing the entire plan for selecting and training the Guard, and establishing a network of Nobby sentinels. The safety net they will provide shall enfold the kingdom within half another fortnight. Please note that these young sentinels placed in strategic vantage points will be trained as silent observers and be paired with eagles and owls. Their role is to observe and notify, never to engage!

"The final element of the plan is most difficult, but it is the centerpiece. It is long term and visionary. We must build a castle, a huge fortress to serve not only as a symbol of Nobby strength, skill, and science, but also as the seat of government, the center of commerce, and, if need be, a sanctuary in the event of outside aggression. Should you share this vision, it would be the greatest single task ever undertaken in Nobby history. It would require total dedication, tremendous effort, and team work to such a degree, Nobbies everywhere would become one heart, one mind, and one body. My question to you is: Can it be done?"

Spirits soared. Voices could be heard around the square. "King Theodore is right! Knowledge is power! We are not defenseless! It makes sense to improve security by improving the flow of information. This is not an impossible dream! The sharper our eyes, the greater the warning, the more lead-time to act, and the greater is the degree of safety. Yes, Nobbies are peace loving! Yes, the Royal Guard is a great idea! Yes, there ought to be a castle in the Kingdom of Thistledom! Yes! Yes! Yes!"

King Theodore was asked to lead, and lead he would. In but a few brief moments, he had lifted their spirits from the bog to the heavens, from the floor of the tavern to his own shoulders. As the meeting ended, words like harmony, synergy, and progress were on every lip. There was nothing Nobbies couldn't do!

King Theodore's father-in-law, Councilor Adrian, immediately agreed to take charge of regional resources and to identify artisans throughout the kingdom. When the castle location was selected, he would prepare the site, work with the Elders to build access trails, and then handle all materials and supplies. The Elders unanimously committed to provide whatever special resources would be required from their own regions.

Bo quietly left the meeting through a side door. He marveled at Theo's ability to read the need and touch their hearts. His vision for the future was bold and exciting. Theo's earlier recommendation to use the seasons of *Shiver* and *Awakening* for planning was a good one. After all, building a castle is not an everyday affair.

In the solitude of his private sanctuary, Bo reflected on all that was said. It would take time to complete the design, and the design couldn't really begin until a location was set. These were two big open issues. He could help Theo with both. Building materials also would depend upon location. It would be a huge task just to gather them—and at this point, materials were not identified either. Plenty of wood and stone were available, but what other elements would be required? Finally, labor would be most important. Skilled artisans lived throughout the kingdom, but they would need tremendous added support from animal friends. There was so much to do. Bo climbed slowly to his loft. The Elders were departing from the front entrance. Bo could hear their excitement. He smiled proudly. Yes, there certainly was much to do.

The periods of *Colors* and *Fire* passed more quickly than ever. It was a time of discovery. Councilor Adrian took charge now as the newly appointed Chancellor of the Kingdom. He shared fully the vision of King Theodore and vowed to make every detail of the plan work. He began by appointing four Vice-Chancellors to head the four provinces: Faba, Kora, Ogle, and Thistle. Each Vice-Chancellor headed a Provincial Council composed of regional representatives who worked closely with area delegates and families. This close-knit organization within the kingdom helped everyone share the vision. By the end of *Fire*, Chancellor Adrian had detailed reports on the entire kingdom: all building materials, names and skills of local artisans, planned output from all the various mines, estimates of food supplies and locations of new storage areas, as well as a survey of important animal and insect populations. King Theodore was pleased with the progress.

Delegations moved quickly and frequently within and between the provinces to determine supply routes and special transportation needs. Having the Royal Guard in place watching over the trails put all at ease. Their uniforms matched the colors of the season and lookout perches were so well hidden, it was next to impossible to spot them. Thistledom's borders were quiet and secure. Nobby pride and self-confidence was at an all-time high as everyone began to pull together.

Throughout *Colors*, *Fire*, and now *Wind*, Bo worked quietly in his lab. What had begun as several different unrelated projects were now meshing into one: How to build an invisible impenetrable fortress? His examination of the rock-hard piece of wood had been the first step. It was indeed wood, or at least it had been. He discovered that air rots old wood, breaking down the fibers. Apparently, the rock-hard wood from the bog never really decayed. Why? Bo concluded it must have been buried eons ago in the mud and clay of the bog. Covered with dirt and water, little or no air reached it. Instead, tiny elements from the ground and sand mixed with the water and then slowly saturated the wood. Over time, these sandy deposits completely filled every tiny space within the wood of the tree and encased the entire outside as well. The dead tree still looked like a wooden tree, but was instead, the much heavier, harder, and stronger rockwood. Bo realized that use of such a strong material would be helpful in building the castle. Only three problems! Could enough be found? Could it be moved? Could it be cut? *How to find out "yes" answers to all three questions?*

Bo knew a giant old rockwood tree lay on its side on the shore of Trogg Island. Perhaps it contained enough wood by itself to make beams and other parts for the entire castle. Perhaps they could find a second tree. After all, the bog was huge. Troggs could be a problem during recovery, but he knew they did leave the island. More must be learned about their behavior and migration patterns.

Assuming that an opportunity would arise to remove the old tree, how might they do it? Rockwood doesn't float, and it would be impossible to move the whole tree in one piece. It was far too heavy! They must be able to cut it. Divided into smaller sections, a combination of deer power, ropes, and either rafts or sleds could do the trick. There wouldn't be much time, however. So the fundamental problem was most clear: How do you cut rockwood? It would take nearly the entire period of *Wind* to find a solution.

The clear salt-like material and strange grains of sand discovered earlier were still the hardest material Bo had found. Harder even than the rockwood. Bo discovered that all the materials had something in common. If scratched cleanly by one of the sharper salt-like rocks, which he now called crystals, a single, well-placed blow would break the material cleanly along the scratch. This worked especially well for cuts that crossed the grain of the rockwood, but not for cuts along the grain. So only half the problem was solved. Cutting across the grain, he could trim limbs off the tree and even cut the thick trunk into smaller sections. That was not enough! He had to find a way to cut along the grain so long beams could be fashioned from the rockwood.

Happily, Bo's earlier research contained another key. The mixture of sand, resin, and thistle seed oil that produced the hard sticky glue used earlier against the hornets could be altered. By changing slightly the amount of resin and oil mixed together, he could reduce the stickiness, and thinning the mixture didn't hurt the glue quality. It still bonded the grains of sand together just as strong as before, making it impossible to break apart or to separate the grains. This didn't seem so important at first, but then Bo got another idea. What if he took thistledown thread… and wound it together with some really strong thread spun by field spiders...and then coated the combination with this new glue sprinkled with some of the grains of crystal sand? *What if...?* He tried it, and the result was amazing. The strands of thread became stiff and sharp. When stretched tightly as a string between two saw handles, the thread cut through ordinary wood like it was warm honey. This new cutting thread was amazing.

Bo's mind raced ahead to a new question: *Would this new thread cut rockwood?* The answer came quickly as he cut a small slice from the piece of rockwood handle. It was easy. Bo remembered, however, the size of that old tree on Trogg Island. How could he cut along the grain of such a huge trunk to make beams and rafters? Cutting through that much material by hand would take too much time, even if it were possible. Keeping a straight line would be difficult too. A simple back and forth cutting motion would not do. It would take forever.

It was during sleep when another idea surfaced. So simple and clear, it jolted him from his bed. He had been dreaming about Troggs and doogles when his thoughts suddenly wandered to an earlier challenge—the hornets. He remembered Theo describing those final moments in the tree and how the nest vibrated under his feet. Theo could *hear* and *feel* the hornets buzzing.

In a flash of insight, Bo imagined two giant beehives on level ground about forty to eighty leaves apart. (He would use bees because they were more friendly and easier to control than hornets. They also made a much louder buzzing sound within the hive.) He would build

## DuBois Castle—The Vision

wooden frames to enclose the hives completely. However, the two sides of the hives facing each other would be covered with something else, and it had to be very soft and thin. He needed a skin-like covering. But what? After several dead ends, he recalled that bark from the birch tree grows by slowly forming many thin layers to serve as skin for the tree. Earlier Nobbies had used this bark as writing tablets.

Bo looked up from his work just in time to see Prince Alec sneaking around the corner of his workshop.

Alec was like his own son in his quiet demeanor, love of science, and passion for problem solving. He had his mother's fine features and love of music, and his golden hair was just like his father's. His mild temperament, self-confidence, and studious nature, however, seemed to flow directly from Uncle Bo. The two surely were kindred spirits, and at this time, neither could have known how their warm friendship would serve and shape the destiny of Thistledom.

"Hi, Uncle Bo! What are you doing?"

"I'm stripping bark off this tree limb."

"Why do you need the bark?"

"Come here. Look carefully at this piece. See how it has many thin layers hidden underneath this white rough part on the outside? These layers are the real skin of the tree."

"Okay! But what are you going to do with them?"

"I need to peel them apart very carefully—like this—and then soak them overnight in thistle seed oil."

"Why? Doesn't the oil make them real squishy?"

Bo smiled. "Yes, it does make them real squishy, but it also makes them soft—just like your skin. If we don't soak them in oil, the air makes them dry and brittle. They would break up in your hands just like dried leaves. We don't want that to happen."

"What are you going to do with them?"

"Come over to my other bench and I'll show you. Would you like to help? I need some good strong hands!"

"Oh yes! Can I please?"

Bo unwrapped a pile of birch skin soaked earlier. They had drained and were still very soft and pliable. He placed several pieces side by side, got a needle and thread, and began to sew the edges together making larger sheets.

Prince Alec held the pieces firmly so Uncle Bo could sew faster. They made three of these larger sheets. Bo then placed them on top of each other carefully staggering and overlapping the seams. Prince Alec held them together while uncle stitched around the edges.

"What do we do next, Uncle Bo?"

"Can you bring the three birch skins we just sewed together over here? Put this end on the top of this frame. Hold on tight! Don't let go! Now, help me stretch the rest of it over this big wooden frame."

As they tugged and pulled the birch skin over the frame, the tension fused the three separate layers into one. Bo secured it in place with clamps and then handed Prince Alec a stick.

"Here! Bang on the birch skin and see what happens. Don't poke it with the end of the stick! Hit it with the flat side."

Prince Alec swung the stick mightily, and the birch skin became a big drum. Everything looked good. It was time for the next step. Earlier Bo had moved two beehives into a storage area along side the lab. The warmer air inside woke the bees and they were anxious to fly out of the hive, but he had covered the entrance.

"Alec, help me place these wooden frames over the hives. Let's stretch the other birch skin over the second frame. Now watch what happens."

The buzzing sound coming from inside the hives bounced against the birch skin and made it vibrate. Alec touched it. The shaking skin tickled his hand. Bo was convinced the rest of the plan would work as well. He attached a long cutting thread to the birch skins on both hives and then stretched it between them. The thread picked up the vibrations from the birch skins and magnified them even more. He realized that the vibrating motion created thousands of tiny cutting strokes that could cut many times faster and with greater precision than cutting by hand. It had worked perfectly in his mind. After several experiments with his small piece of rockwood and a few minor adjustments, it worked at his lab too. Now that he knew the rockwood building material could be cut and shaped, it was time to visit with Theo about the castle site. Bo smiled as he thought to himself, *Wait until Theo sees this!*

It seemed impossible! The *Festival of Light* again was just two days hence. This cycle of seasons had passed quicker than any before. Bo reflected. *So much had happened: The discovery of Trogg Island; the close call with the Troggs; establishment of the Royal Guard; the appointment of Chancellor Adrian and the new organization of the Kingdom; all the talk about the castle; my own discoveries. Perhaps that's why time passed so quickly. So much happening in such a short time. It would be very difficult to pull King Theodore away from festival activities. He and Astrid are in great demand. Mother will have to help.*

The Royal family met at its customary breakfast to begin the Shortest Day. The Festival was always so exciting. Prince Alec was beginning to display athletic ability inherited from his father and was eager to participate in some of the games. He also volunteered to be a judge for the baking contest—well at least he could be a royal taster. As usual, the contests and events would continue throughout the day and early evening. After the beam of the North Star appeared, the Royal Ball would begin in the main hall of the tavern. There was a lot to do. Bo caught Theo's eye at the end of breakfast. They remained at the table while Irene, Astrid, and Alec left to prepare for the festivities.

"What is it, Bo?"

"Tonight after the opening ceremonies at the ball, can you leave for awhile?"

"Yes, I suppose I can. But why?"

"It has to do with the site for the castle."

"Can I look at the plans later?"

"No, Theo. Not the plans! I want you to see the site."

King Theodore was surprised. He knew that Chancellor Adrian had been meeting with the Provincial Councils to discuss possible sites, but none had been chosen. Actually, they were to review findings right after the Festival. Bo noted the puzzled look and smiled warmly.

"Mother and I have talked, and she agrees wholeheartedly. This is the perfect site for the castle."

"Mother has seen the site?"

"Yes! In fact, it is her idea. And it's a marvelous idea!"

"Does Chancellor Adrian know? Has he seen it?"

"No! Only Mother and I have seen it—and Dad."

"What? Dad?"

King Theodore suddenly recalled the mysterious trip Bo and his parents had taken during the Festival many cycles earlier. He never did know where they had gone. His curiosity was aroused. Bo never ceased to amaze him. He was always full of surprises. Puzzlement turned to excitement.

"Okay, brother, I'm ready! Can we go now?"

"No, Theo, we must wait until dark—after the beam appears. I'll get everything ready. Meet me outside behind my lab right after your welcoming remarks. We'll be gone several hours. Be sure to bring a jacket and scarf. Don't worry! Mom will explain everything to Astrid and

## DuBois Castle—The Vision

cover for us at the ball. And, Theo, say nothing about this to anyone. It must remain between us for the moment."

It was the first day of *Snow*, the beginning of the *Shiver* season, the Festival of Light, and the Shortest Day of the cycle. But for King Theodore, it was the longest day of his life. He hated waiting.

Bo watched from his balcony as the beam of the North Star reappeared beginning a new cycle. It was indeed a remarkable sight, but paled in comparison to what Theo was about to see. Bo's thoughts raced far ahead. *Some day perhaps all Nobbies could bathe in that soothing glow. What better place for the royal castle than to stand always in this wondrous light from above. And if the castle were drenched in this light, what other wonders might follow? Could the power of the beam be used for greater good? The beam was beautiful, but did it have practical uses as well? Could its marvelous energy be captured and stored? What if...*

Bo's thoughts were interrupted by the rustle of a lone figure moving quickly through the shadows below. It was Theo. He was early. No matter, everything was ready. Bo grabbed a long black and green scarf as he hurried back through the doorway and down the stairs. Theo was already at the bottom.

"Okay, Bo, I'm ready! Let's go!"

Bo led the way to the back of the lab. There in a small clearing stood two old friends, the owls that had carried them earlier to and from Trogg Island. They lowered their heads as Bo and Theo approached, but no guide ropes were needed. The brothers climbed aboard, and with quick powerful strokes, the owls rose above the trees. Circling the tavern once, they headed straight North—directly toward the beam.

As so often happens, the night of the Shortest Day was cold and clear. No clouds. No wind. Countless stars spilled over the horizons, like grains of light floating in an endless ocean of black. In the distance was the widening beam of the North Star, a marvelous and mysterious shaft of light linking the heavens and the earth. Theo stared in wonder. Bo rode silently alongside. No words could describe the immensity surrounding them.

Bo guided the owls to a spot near the trees where they could hear water flowing from the mountain. It was very near the top. They could see the beam shining down the opposite side of the peak. Bo knew the large granite stage was just ahead beyond the rise leading to the other side. Theo heard the water splashing on the rocks and walked toward it.

"No, Theo, follow me!"

Bo moved quickly along the familiar path leading away from the stream. On this side of the peak away from the beam, it was dark, very steep, and filled with loose

## DuBois Castle—The Vision

shale. Theo hurried to catch up. As they reached a plateau and rounded the bend, there it was. The beam of the North Star lit the entire area. Theo was stunned! The reality of seeing the very spot of the beam was beyond imagination. It defied belief. Surely, his eyes were deceiving him. It was an illusion!

Bo walked into the light and motioned Theo to follow. He hesitated. Bo raised his arms toward the heavens. The light was so soothing. Again, he waved at Theo to come into the light. Theo stood firm, as if in a trance, his senses overwhelmed. Finally, he saw Bo's eyes, now turned blue in the golden glow, peering back at him. This was such a strange, unexpected sight. Finally, Bo came over, took his arm, and led him into the light. They spent the rest of the night sitting face to face basking in the warmth of the beam and discussing the dream they would build together. King Theodore learned much about his father, his brother, and Nobby history.

It was first light when the owls returned to the tree near the stream to begin the homeward journey. Within seconds, their huge powerful wings were riding the air currents once again. Looking at the ground below, Bo realized they were not far from Trogg Island. The bog was just off to the left. Unable to resist, they dropped lower for a closer look.

There were many island thickets, many more than they had seen earlier from the tree line. Trogg huts were easy to spot now that they knew where to look. There was not one Trogg Island either, but a whole neighborhood of islands. Theo was surprised to see so many scattered across the bog. The one they had visited was closest to the mainland and also happened to be the largest. It was strange! There were no camp fires. No signs of activity. The Troggs were gone again, but where?

It had been a very busy night and dawn was now in full bloom. They were tired, and Bo knew the owls were already overdue at their nesting trees. They headed straight toward Thistleville. It didn't take long. Bo and Theo shared a warm fire and hot tea. Now that the site was selected, plans and work on the castle could begin immediately. King Theodore said he would tell the Council about the location. The true nature of the site, however, should remain secret until later—much later. Bo agreed.

Throughout the season of *Shiver*, King Theodore and Bo worked on design ideas for the castle. High ground, bird's eye view, and water were already present, so they worked on ways to make best use of the natural resources. Other natural benefits, like the large granite stage area and how it lay hidden in a nook high up on the western side of the mountain, were also important factors. King Theodore wanted to make full use of every advantage. After all, this would not be just any castle, but a castle-fortress to protect all future generations of Nobbies. The safety of citizens now and forever more would be the responsibility of the King. Many nightlong planning sessions followed. The loft over Bo's lab was the favorite spot.

It was King Theodore's idea to use the large natural stage area as a central courtyard for the castle and to build high surrounding walls at the outer edges using the granite as a foundation. Camouflage was his top priority. He insisted that the castle have a strategic view, but at the same time, remain hidden from prying eyes. The key to future Nobby security would be the ability to live in secrecy—undetected by Troggs or any other potential adversaries. They would see and remain unseen!

This concern for concealment led King Theodore to use the mountain, itself, as part of the castle. Workers had discovered that the granite forming the natural stage area was just a single thin layer. There were other layers deeper in the ground separated by earth and clay. A large cavern holding a huge underground lake—the source of the stream flowing out of the rocks—was also found. The water was pure and clear as the cold night air. Indeed, the site of the castle was filled with natural wonders.

After studying new drawings and charts of the mountain, King Theodore saw a great opportunity. If stonecutters could punch holes through the various layers of granite at select locations, miners could carve out many separate underground living levels. Once excavated, each level could be converted to hold guest chambers. More levels and guest rooms could be added as needed almost indefinitely. By using this space within the mountain, most of the castle could be safely tucked underground where the temperature would remain constant, unaffected by the changing seasons above ground. Hidden entrances and a network of tunnels leading from all sides of the mountain to the castle would provide easy and safe access to Nobbies coming from any direction. Bo liked the plan and offered several ways to make air shafts and to transfer light from the surface throughout all the underground levels. He had no doubt. They could do it!

That part of the castle to be built in the open above ground would also require special planning. Because it would stand in a large hollow in the side of the mountaintop, the use of natural materials like rock, wood, and stone was essential. If built correctly using random placement of stones and vines, the castle would blend into the terrain becoming invisible from the valleys below. King Theodore drew the main plans, which showed seven levels above ground. Several of these, however, were further subdivided into three separate floors in some areas. There were large gathering halls, small meeting rooms, dining areas, and a private section set aside as royal chambers. King Theodore also designed a system of secret passage ways and hidden staircases. Should the castle, itself, ever be overrun, this labyrinth would provide a final avenue of escape.

As you can see, great attention was given to conceal the castle structure both inside and out. But if camouflage failed, the castle would need the strength of a fortress. Bo had plans for this as well, and the key would be beams and shutters made from the rockwood tree in the bog.

King Theodore's master plan also included high towers at each end of the castle extending just over the crest of the mountain. These vantage points would give a clear view of the entire countryside in every direction.

## DuBois Castle—The Vision

Early detection and advance warning were important elements in King Theodore's security scheme.

As a final precaution, he also envisioned a moat around the exposed side of the castle. It would be created by digging a trench and shoring the outer bank with stone and clay removed earlier in the underground excavation phase. When the trench was completed, the stream flowing out one side of the mountain could be diverted to fill the moat, and then returned to the underground lake on the other side. The towers and moat were very important, but King Theodore knew in his heart they were much longer-term projects. There was much to do before they could ever begin. Sighing, he looked toward the heavens. "Why me?"

"Lord Norbert, when did they start the castle?"

"How many Nobbies worked on it?"

"How long did it take?"

"Did Bo's thread cutter really cut the rockwood?"

"How did they get the big rockwood tree all the way from Trogg Island? Did the Troggs see them?"

"Did Alec win any of the competitions?"

Lord Norbert looked quickly around the room and began to laugh. He laughed loud and long. It was just like old times. Nothing had really changed. The royal cousins had as many questions now as when they were tiny children. Princess Emily started laughing too. Then Ellen and Paul. Shortly, the whole room rocked with laughter. It was funny. Lord Norbert talked for an hour and no one had made a sound. As soon as he stopped, the room went crazy with questions. Lord Norbert certainly did have a way with words. It was good to be together again. Finally, Prince Aaron, the eldest of the cousins, got everyone's attention: "Lord Norbert, you must admit that these are very good questions. Do you have the answers? We'll go crazy if you don't."

"Yes, Aaron, I do. But first, how about a little more tea?"

Julia was first off her chair. She poured a generous cup and placed it next to Lord Norbert with a little honey and laughed. "Here it is, Lord Norbert! This should help the words flow even smoother!"

He gave her a quick hug and a wink. Lord Norbert gazed intently at the floor for a brief moment. "A cookie for your thoughts," Emily quipped.

Lord Norbert looked up and just smiled. He was very old and very wise, and it was clear to all that tonight, he was very happy. There was no place he would rather be.

He raised his hands, took a very deep breath, and began to divulge stories never heard before. Stories that would answer many questions but raise even more. The children would not only get a glimpse of their precious history, but also begin to live with puzzling mysteries of the past yet to be unraveled.

## DuBois Castle—Fruition

R esources was the buzz word when *Shiver* season came. King Theodore and Bo worked unceasingly throughout its entirety. Thankfully, they were not alone. Chancellor Adrian, all four Vice Chancellors, and Provincial Councils organized the entire kingdom into a single-minded work team. The first goal: Preparation. Get all the excavation and construction resources needed to the site. Identify all the special skills required and form work teams of specialists. Organize backup support and systems for necessities like food, water, shelter, medical attention, and transportation.

    The Royal Guard became even more important now. Since it took much longer to move supplies and resources along the trails, Nobbies were more exposed to outside dangers for longer periods of time. Frequently, they moved in large groups using many animals. The role of the Guard was crucial to their safety—especially during the daring removal of the rockwood tree from the bog. How did they do it?

Apparently, Troggs left their island huts during *Shiver* taking nearly everything with them. They were certainly gone during *Ice*. With the bog frozen solid, except for the deepest areas, it was easy to get to Trogg Island. Bo worked with his life-long friend, Cecil, to train a herd of deer. They rode the deer back and forth between the island and the mainland until a pathway across the ice and snow was trampled smooth. This was the first step.

Teams of tree-cutters and woodcarvers from Thistle cleared ice, snow, and sand away from the giant rockwood. This took several days of hard work. Using Bo's special coated cutting threads and some of the sharp crystals, they began to score the limbs. Once all the measuring and marking were completed, they erected a large tripod made from the hardwood of a chestnut tree. The three wooden poles were movable and positioned so the legs would straddle the limb to be cut. A long, heavy battering ram with a pointed edge resembling the head of an ax was suspended from the top point of the tripod so it would swing freely in the center area between the three poles. When all was ready, Cecil would hook a large buck to the end of the battering ram, pull it back slowly, and then pull a slipknot in the rope sending the ram smashing into the limb. If scored properly and if the aim was good, the limb broke clean through after a single hit. With each successful cut, the deer hauled the rockwood across the frozen bog, up the bank, and then along a winding trail to the castle site.

It took eight days and nights to cut and haul just the limbs. The tree trunk posed special problems. It was important to keep the cut sections as large as possible in order to make longer one-piece support beams. Cutting larger sections, however, was not the problem. It was moving them. These heavy sections could be pulled easily across the hard ice, but gouged the frozen ground when the deer started moving up the trail. To solve the problem, Chancellor Adrian had metalworkers and blacksmiths from Faba hammer out flat sheets of copper. The trunk sections were rolled onto these sheets, secured with ropes, and then a team of eight large deer completed the task. The load was still very heavy but slid easily along the frozen ground. Sharp wooden stakes were pounded into the ground through slots at the back end of the copper sleds whenever the deer rested during the long climb to the top. This prevented the sled and the heavy rockwood section from sliding back down the mountain trail.

Hundreds of Nobbies worked together with the deer to remove the rockwood tree from the bog. It was a dangerous task. The work was exhausting for Nobbies and the deer. Ironically, the tree was not as heavy as the weight of worry over the possible return of the Troggs. To help alleviate the worry, the Royal Guard extended its network of lookout points all the way to the far edge of the bog. Its collective eye saw every movement. Thanks to the Guard, the entire tree was moved in secrecy and safety. A heavy snowfall quickly erased all evidence of the trail across the ice and up the bank. The Troggs would never know.

## DuBois Castle—Fruition

The huge granite stage nearly disappeared under the blanket of supplies and the many building materials carried to the site. Chancellor Adrian had designated separate storage areas for stone, wood, and rockwood. Mining equipment, fire pits, cutting tools, sawmill, and drilling tools were located around the perimeter. Areas for food and tents were chosen near the stream. A whole village rose from the ground just for the miners coming from Faba and Ogle. Other areas were set up for stonecutters, woodcutters and carvers, and hundreds of other artisans eager to work on the castle. Several spots just a bit lower on the mountainside were also specially prepared for the work animals. Chancellor Adrian knew the entire site and everything on and around it. He would make sure everything was ready when the King gave the royal command: "It is time! Let the building begin!"

The first day of *Buds* began the wondrous season of *Awakening*. With new life bursting forth, a new spirit filled the Land. It was the day chosen as the symbolic beginning of DuBois Castle. A glorious day! King Theodore issued a proclamation formally announcing the site and committing the collective heart and mind of the kingdom to the task. Because of the limited access, he asked that only those directly involved as workers or support teams come to the site. Chancellor Adrian made good on his promise. All supplies, materials, and tools were ready.

As a ceremonial first step, King Theodore delivered the very first hammer blow to the layer of granite that would become the foundation for everything. What a blow it was! Still unaware of the truly epic size of the task he was beginning, the sound would reverberate down the mountainside, through the valleys and bogs, and then echo throughout the kingdom for three generations. He stood straight and tall, laid the hammer down, and nodded his head in satisfaction. His broad smile energized the crowd. There would be no more work done this day. This was a moment to celebrate and remember. It was the pivotal point in Nobby history.

Days and weeks passed; the work never stopped. Soon *Suntime* and *Color* passed. Time seemed but a wink of the eye. Never had Nobbies worked so hard and enjoyed it more. There was purpose in every move, satisfaction with each shovel of earth removed, and love in every load brought to the surface. Every action built the dream, turning possibilities into plans and darkness into light. Moles, ferrets, badgers, and wolverines helped dig, loosen, and remove buckets of earth and stone. Thanks to Bo, the animals worked in complete harmony with each other and their Nobby teams.

Stonecutters broke through the granite layer at the critical spots marked by King Theodore himself. This opened up access to the earth and sand strata beneath the granite. These initial shafts were then used to determine reference points and mark the various depths of the five major underground levels. Each major level would be four zygs high, and in turn, further subdivided into five smaller levels. These would become the corridors built to house all the individual living chambers.

At the same time, other miners from Faba and Ogle competed in the excavation of two separate tunnels, each one zyg square and about 250 zygs long, coming from separate sides of the mountain. These would become the main but secret underground corridors leading from the outside all the way to the Grand Gathering Hall beneath the great granite stage—soon to be the courtyard. All other corridors housing private chambers would branch off from these two central passages and lead away from the Hall like spokes in a wheel. Staircases and a series of slides connected the many levels. Four large caverns, thirty zygs square, were carved out on this main level right beneath the granite, carefully leaving untouched, sixteen huge sections of earth and rock, three zygs square. These sections became the pillars at the corners of each large cavern. These pillars would also serve as support columns for the future courtyard and castle above. This main underground level would be the largest and provide for stores and shops, a central bakery and kitchens, library, and eventually, even a Nobby hospital.

In order to save time and reduce mistakes, King Theodore set up a Castle Planning Committee. Its main role was to look at long-range plans for the castle and grounds. The first task was deciding what to do with the earth and stone that was removed to make the underground portion of the castle. There was a lot! They certainly did not want to move it twice! After only one meeting, they had a plan. Much of it would be hauled immediately away from the site to form a natural roadway through the dense forest on the top third of the mountain. Most, however, would be spread evenly, layer upon layer, around the area perimeter. This mound would later become the outer bank of the moat. This indeed would be an engineering marvel to behold.

Bo was asked to head this committee. He also took personal charge for developing the ventilation system and his own plan to light the entire subterranean area. Air and light were critical elements. Without them, the underground plans for the castle would not work. Bo assured Theodore and the committee that his plans for both systems would work. No one doubted his word.

As the *Color* season ended and the Shortest Day approached once again to usher in the time of *Shiver*, King Theodore and Bo talked about the beam and the need to keep their secret a bit longer. King Theodore had an answer. He would host the first Royal DuBois Ball back at the tavern in Thistleville. Everyone working on the castle would attend. It was perfect! And to celebrate the unbelievable success of their early efforts, everyone would wear work clothes. No finery! Just everyday work clothes! As a matter of fact, the Ball would be dedicated to the dignity, power, and nobility of the Nobby spirit. Without it, a castle was not possible.

Word spread quickly. It was a great idea! Everyone surely was ready to party. Much had been accomplished. It was time to rest and to celebrate. And so they did. Chancellor Adrian set up villages of tents surrounding Thistleville. There was room for everyone. A special warmth filled Nobby hearts as the beam appeared. It marked the first cycle that Nobbies had their very own castle—even though it was still more a dream than reality. The dream, however, was real and so was their progress. Theo and Bo smiled warmly as they toasted DuBois

## DuBois Castle—Fruition

Castle. They looked out at the beam and knew exactly what it really marked—the castle and the future.

Two more cycles passed without much outward change at the site. Below ground was another story! Accommodations to house a very large village were completed. Stores and shops already were providing goods and services and several kitchens and a bakery now fed the workers. Excavation and construction of the underground phase was ahead of schedule because weather was not a factor. The temperature remained constant, and once main corridors, stairways, and slides were complete, the pace of work moved faster and faster as one success fed upon another.

Bo's plans for ventilation worked very well. Remember that the two main tunnels leading to the Grand Gathering Hall at the center of the first underground level came from the two sides of the mountain. The entrances were large enough, but very well hidden. When opened, wind coming from either direction created a natural flow of fresh air throughout the entire underground structure. Several vertical shafts served much like chimney drafts to remove stale air that was forced up and out by the periodic opening and closing of the doors at the two main passageways. As hundreds of individual private chambers were completed, Nobby artisans and workers moved from the tents along the stream to the security and comfort inside the new DuBois Castle below.

The lighting scheme was quite ingenious. Bo had worked closely with miners from Kora to secure large quantities of those hard crystals—in all different sizes. Ferrets and moles dug several shafts, each angling away from a central chamber built just above the Gathering Hall ceiling and just below the granite courtyard above. As the sun moved daily across the sky, its rays shone through these openings into the chamber. Even on cloudy days, sunlight was captured and stored in thousands of crystals packed tightly, and encased in a large frame lined with coal. Bo also stored huge amounts of light energy from another source, but that remained a secret for the time being.

Thousands of tiny crystals were strung on a special thread coated with crystal dust and then stretched throughout the entire underground structure. Using the crystals and a series of mirrors, Bo was able to transmit light to every room on every level. The light was controlled by placing a small disk coated with coal dust at any place along the thread to interrupt the transfer of light from one crystal to the next. Sliding the disk outward away from the thread would let increasing amounts of light pass. The light was soft, easy on the eyes, and produced no heat. Progress on all fronts was great, and it seemed the longer they worked, the faster the pace would grow.

It had taken three full cycles to complete the entire underground phase of the castle—a truly remarkable achievement. Perhaps even more notable was the fact that nothing interfered with the work. The Royal Guard maintained its silent vigil without incident. Travel throughout the Kingdom was safe. Materials and supplies moved rapidly. Not a single Nobby was threatened or lost.

## DuBois Castle—Fruition

Vigilance and prevention remained key elements in King Theodore's mind. He reminded all to travel along only approved routes. As construction began on the visible part of the castle, there was greater likelihood that they would be noticed. Accordingly, the Castle Committee decided that perimeter walls and gates should be built next—before the castle, itself.

The plans for outer walls followed the edges of the large layer of granite in order to use it as a foundation. Rocks, fieldstone, and slate were the building blocks held together by a mixture of sand, thistleseed flour, crystal dust, and pine resin. Deer helped turn large wooden mixing blades in a large pit carved from the granite to make this special mortar. As soon as the base of the walls was completed, crews planted vines and wild berry bushes alongside so they would later climb the stone and provide a natural covering. The walls, of course, would protect workers and the vines would help conceal the later construction of the castle, itself. Only trees and shrubs hindering construction of the wall were cut. All others remained to provide further protective cover and to help deaden the sound of hammers pounding against chisels.

Make no mistake! Building the perimeter walls was a monumental task. The Castle Committee met to determine ways to become more efficient. It decided to clean and cut smaller stones below the granite courtyard in a corner of the Great Gathering Hall. Many Nobbies worked here in day and night shifts. The ringing of hammer blows was muffled, weather was never a factor, and rocks and stones could be processed much faster.

Speed was most important because King Theodore wanted a wall four zygs high and one zyg wide. Considering that the entire perimeter of the wall was two hundred forty zygs long including a two zygs wide main gate, thousands and thousands of stones were required. Lifts powered by deer hoisted finished stones to the surface, and then teams of wolverines and badgers pulled cart after cart to the workers at the walls. Two more cycles passed before members of the Royal Guard took their stations at lookout perches high atop the completed walls. It was quite a sight! The only holidays taken during the past five cycles had been at the *Festival of Light* celebrated in Thistleville and the Longest Day at the beginning of *Suntime*. No one complained. Nobby artisans and workers were totally dedicated and committed to building the dream called DuBois Castle. The secret of the beam, however, remained.

In recognition of the achievements at the castle site, King Theodore proclaimed the entire period of *Sun* as a time of rest and relaxation, a time of celebration and renewal. Workers returned to their families and villages throughout the kingdom. The size and wonders of the castle walls and underground chambers grew with each retelling. Those who worked at the site were much admired. It was something families would boast about for generations. For every Nobby returning home, three wanted to come back with them to the site. Everyone wanted to help! DuBois Castle truly was becoming the symbolic home of all Nobbies.

"Father, I have finished my formal schooling. If it's okay with you and Mom, I would like to begin working on the castle construction with the different guilds and crafts. I want to know how to do all these things with my own hands."

"Alec, your mother would never permit it. It's too dangerous!"

"I will be seventeen soon! Isn't our family responsible for the well-being of all in the kingdom?"

"Yes, we are! What does this have to do with your working with all the tradesmen?"

"If we are to lead, we must know and understand as much as possible. I want to learn by doing! Doesn't this make sense? I will be careful. Uncle Bo and Grandfather Adrian can set it up. You can explain it to Mom. She always listens to you! Besides, I like working with my hands!"

"Okay! But I want to see the plan you work out with your uncle and grandfather *before* you begin. Does this make sense to you?"

"Agreed! Thank you."

Artisans and workers returned to the mountain on the third day of *Heat* and construction on the castle, itself, finally began.

Foundations for fireplaces and the outer castle walls transformed the granite staging area into the main floor of DuBois Castle. At this time, the courtyard area became one giant woodworking shop. Large saws stood ready to fashion beams and support braces for ceilings, interior walls, and staircases. Woodcarvers began work on banisters, railings, and doors. Others designed and carved decorative panels for the Throne Room and Great Dining Hall. Still others concentrated on elaborate moldings for ceilings and doorways. Trees removed from the site and roadway were transformed into works of art reflecting the imagination and grace of the Nobby spirit. Nothing was wasted. Most exciting, however, was the setup of Bo's rockwood cutting tool.

After dinner one evening, Bo sketched a diagram of his idea and gave it the next morning to the Carpenters and Woodworkers Guild so work on the giant saw could begin immediately. Carpenters were to construct four huge wooden frames that could be placed two-by-two lengthwise. The diagram set the inside dimensions at five zygs long, two zygs wide, and eight thistle leafs (lfs) high. The frames would be connected by large wooden dowels placed across the middle span and by strong rope strapping along the center space. Laying flat on the ground, the four frames would serve as a platform base to hold the largest rockwood limbs so they could be cut lengthwise.

The diagram also required woodworkers to fashion thirty large posts two zygs long and six lfs in diameter from oak logs. When completed, workers shortened the posts by two lfs, and then drilled center holes (one lf diameter and six lfs deep) into both ends. When the posts were completed, metalworkers and blacksmiths fitted both ends of each post with a metal nose-piece. When hoisted into place inside the boxes, posts were held in place with large pins driven through the sides of the boxes into the holes in the post ends. After some initial turning in place with plenty of thistleseed oil applied, the pins and posts spun freely as rollers inside the box frames.

Bo rigged a series of pulleys and winches to raise and lower the assembled box frames from four large hooks placed along each side. When the boxes were raised and tilted toward each other at a thirty-five degree angle, the rope strapping held them together as they formed a giant V-shaped cradle to hold the largest sections of the rockwood tree. Once each rockwood limb was placed in position, it would move into the cutting thread. It was an engineering marvel.

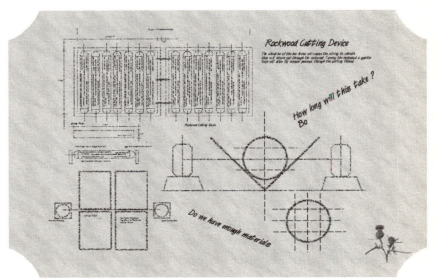

All other work stopped when Bo positioned several beehives at the center opening on both sides of the cradle. After gathering them close together within two large wooden frames, he stretched the cutting thread between the soft white birchskin sides facing each other. The vibrating system and the cutting thread worked perfectly.

"Uncle Bo! I was reviewing your cutting tool diagram last night and I have an idea. If it works, it would save us a lot of time. I explained it to some of the Guild members this morning. They like the idea. Can I show you?"

Uncle Bo was very pleased with the effort and dedication Alec had shown since becoming an apprentice with the carpenters and woodworkers. He was ecstatic with his creative potential as well.

"Terrific! What have you got? Any idea that can speed up cutting rockwood is most welcome!"

"Uncle Bo, the vibrating cutting thread works very well. What if we added two more cutting threads to the system and then attached all three to the birchskins with an adjustable strap? Do you think the hives would provide enough energy to vibrate all of them?"

"I don't know, but we can try it right now! Show me how your strap idea would work and explain how you would use the additional threads."

By mid-afternoon, Alec added a narrow layer of birchskin to the vibrating frames and Uncle Bo stretched and positioned two more threads. Alec asked some of the workers to bring the trunk of a spruce so he could test and demonstrate what would happen. They pulled it into place and lifted the box frames into cradle position. As the winches slowly pulled the trunk into the threads, three simultaneous cuts were made instead of one producing four long sections. After this fist pass, the pieces fell against each other remaining in their original positions. Uncle Bo smiled immediately. Three threads cut as easily as one. Everyone was very excited, but there was more.

"Uncle Bo, watch what happens now! Move the winches to the side of the cradle and roll this entire four-piece trunk exactly one quarter of a turn."

The workers did as instructed and with a little more thistleseed oil, the trunk moved as if it were still a single giant piece.

"Excellent! Uncle Bo, watch what happens as we pull it back through the cutting threads."

This second pass made only three more cuts, but immediately produced a total of sixteen beams: four beams from the center section of the large trunk were cut perfectly square; eight other beams emerged from the four sides of the trunk with bark remaining on one side; and four smaller beams cut in quarter round were also produced that could be used for decorative trim.

"Alec, this is amazing! It's brilliant! Let's make two more cutting tools using smaller hives for finer cuts to make window shutters and interlocking notches in the ends of the larger beams."

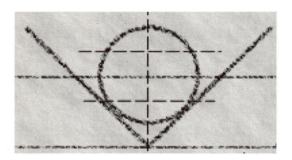

Word of Alec's idea spread like the wind. Although he had not inherited his father's height, his stature certainly had grown in Nobby eyes, as well as in the hearts of his fellow workers that afternoon. He was one of them, and they were very proud to work at his side.

Earlier the Castle Committee had deep concerns about the availability of large construction beams. With the inventions of Bo and Alec, they decided to use the rockwood for the main gate and also as support beams for the front of the castle. Unfortunately, there was not enough for the entire upper levels of the castle. Oak and cherry would be suitable substitutes.

By the time *Shiver* season arrived along with another celebration of the *Festival of Light*, much of the castle frame was in place. Chimneys, however, continued to lead the race toward the sky soaring a full twenty-two zygs. It would take time yet for the exterior walls and finally the roof rafters to close the gap. In contrast to the earlier work underground, weather now determined work speed and progress. The Grand Gathering Hall became a fine arts area filled with oil paintings and large tapestries. Carpenters built tables, chairs, and other furniture for every room. Woodcarvers and sculptors chipped away at decorative murals and panels. Finally, seamstresses cut and sewed curtains, drapes, and table linens. Underground chambers were expanded to provide living quarters for the growing workforce. Lower corridors stored completed items. Two more cycles would pass before shutters adorned the windows and the castle roof finally closed out the sunshine. Alec had produced another marvel as well. He coated the wooden shingles with a special layer of crystal sand, pine resin, corn oil, and coal. It repelled the rain and absorbed light so there would be no reflection seen from afar. DuBois Castle stood tall and proud at the top of a mountain, yet, remained virtually invisible. It was indeed a marvel reflecting the mind and muscle the fueled the Nobby spirit.

Once the castle walls and roof were sealed, seven major levels above ground received final touches. Each of the six levels above the main floor was further subdivided into three, but not in any uniform manner. By staggering the areas subdivided from one level to another, King Theodore was able to create illusions involving space and shapes creating a network of secret passages, hidden staircases, and false ceilings and floors. This final plan for deception was born of his desire to protect succeeding generations of the royal family and to provide avenues of escape should the castle ever be discovered and the outer walls breached by an enemy. It took three added cycles to complete the castle itself.

    Intricately carved panels, tapestries, paintings, clocks, curtains and draperies, furniture, and decorative moldings and beams transformed rooms and halls into places of flowing grace and beauty. The temperature below ground remained constant and comfortable. Heat from kitchens and workshops warmed the main castle through a series of fire-hardened clay ducts made by potters from Faba. The heat rose naturally from the underground area to the top floors of the castle. Duct panels in the attic opened or closed to control air flow to maintain comfortable temperatures. Fireplaces throughout the castle added heat. Furniture filled the castle, transforming it from a huge building into a grand home with a great and warm heart.

# DuBois Castle—Homecoming

The time has arrived, a moment filled with immense happiness and promise yet, tinged with inevitable sadness. The Royal Castle DuBois is finished, but not complete. The Royal Family DuBois is missing. It is time to leave behind the tavern, Bo's loft, and Thistleville, home of a thousand memories and dreams. It is most difficult for Irene. She knows Zygmunt would follow wherever she goes, but their life together has carved such a powerful presence in this place. The public meetings he led, the intimate moments shared there in the warmth and security of their home above the dining hall. It is hard to walk away. His spirit is embedded in every board and breath of air. Bo sits with his mother for a very long time. They hold hands, smile a bit, and cry. But in the end, royalty brings with it an awesome responsibility, which transcends personal desires and even grief. It calls forth leadership and sacrifice. It demands a focus that penetrates beyond the present and far past the pale of Thistleville. It gives birth to a vision extending all the way to the far reaches of the provinces. All are bound by sacred oath and the Kingdom of Thistledom. Bo and his mother stand, embrace, and walk hand in hand from a glorious past to a royal future holding seeds of promise.

The royal family arrived at DuBois Castle a scant three days before the *Festival of Light*. This time, artisans and workers remained for the celebration. Chancellor Adrian, Vice Chancellors, Provincial Council Members, and many local leaders all came to celebrate. This Festival would be the first celebrated at the castle and would mark the official beginning of the Kingdom—now complete with royal family. Nobbies were very proud.

Thousands of visitors took great delight staying in the chambers below and visiting a wondrous underground world. It was hard to believe. All were amazed by Bo's string-lighting, stairways and slides between levels, the shops and stores, and the bakery and kitchens. The castle above ground was a feast for the eyes as well. Nobby art and skills adorned every hall and room, and were never better displayed. Hand carved wood panels in the Throne Room depicting important events in Nobby history were breathtaking—especially the triple life-size figure of Zygmunt astride Binder. The walk through the huge main gate and across the open courtyard ringed with garden walkways and fountains gave the feeling of great security and peace. Nobbies could not get enough of DuBois Castle. It was a grand and beautiful sight! It was bigger than life and boggled the mind.

As daylight waned all thoughts turned to the Castle DuBois Inaugural Ball. Everyone awaited the chance to

## DuBois Castle—Homecoming

see King Theodore and Queen Astrid again. Countless young Nobbesses also awaited the appearance of Prince Alec. With so many guests, however, the dinner feast was moved from the Great Ballroom on the main floor to the larger Grand Gathering Hall beneath the courtyard.

Amid the jealous gaze of thousands of breathless green eyes, Queen Mother Irene entered on the arm of Prince Alec. She was radiant in a beautiful deep green gown trimmed in white lace. Her snow white hair glistened, a glorious crown reflecting the soft colored lights Bo had devised for the evening. She smiled and waved to all as they curtsied and applauded. All knew who she was and what she had meant to Thistledom. It was a rare privilege to be in her presence. A gallant Alec extended his strong right arm gently guiding his grandmother to center stage so she could stand alone in the moment. Truly she had given her life to all of them. They knew it and so did he. It was a proud moment they shared—one neither would forget.

When Alec stepped forward to his grandmother's side, the Grand Gathering Hall erupted in applause and cheering. The sound was deafening. Thousands of Nobbies knew him not only as Prince Alec, heir to the throne, but as a craftsman and fellow Guild member. Hundreds of Nobesses knew him as the handsome prince in their recurring dreams—and handsome he was! This evening, his black waistcoat and britches trimmed in dark green thread, accented by the colored lights, made his long golden hair glow. He walked easily with great grace among many friends that evening. Each one who clasped his strong hands also felt the presence of greatness. It is an intangible extending far beyond the present that defies definition because the feeling cannot be captured with mere words. Greatness springs from within as a spontaneous gift to be shared.

Moments later, King Theodore and Queen Astrid entered. Again the applause and admiration spilled out of the room and throughout the castle. King Theodore, once the symbol of their vision, was now the embodiment of their wildest dreams. He had given them a grand plan and sense of purpose, and they had accepted the challenge and built it. What a night for celebrating!

Chancellor Adrian and his wife, Penette, also entered to warm applause. Their service to the Kingdom was legendary. They, of course were the parents of Queen Astrid, but tonight they were most famous for being the grandparents of Prince Alec.

Without being noticed, Bo had slipped into the Grand Hall through a service entrance. However, Chancellor Adrian was not about to miss the opportunity to recognize him and his tremendous creations. Again the Great Hall exploded with applause and cheers amid a great outpouring of expressions of gratitude and love. King Theodore and Queen Astrid led the applause as Prince Alec and a few coal miner friends from Kora lifted him onto their shoulders. King Theodore knew, as did everyone, that while they represented the head, arms, legs, heart, and muscle of the Kingdom, Bo truly was the soul of Thistledom.

## DuBois Castle—Homecoming

As the applause slowed momentarily, Chancellor Adrian offered a toast to the royal family and the kingdom. He announced that they would dine first and then go to the courtyard directly above to see the beam of the North Star, the first true *Festival of Light* celebration in the Land of Thistledom.

As she held tightly to Prince Alec's hand, Irene shared a warm secret smile with Bo and Theo as their eyes met for but a moment. From his place at the front of the hall and flanked by family and friends, King Theodore saw clearly for the first time the epic grandeur and dimension of his dream. Yes, Thistledom was real and its soaring spirit filled every heart.

At the conclusion of the meal, King Theodore rose and in deep resonant tones tinged with emotion spoke to the assembled family of Thistledom.

"Citizens of Thistledom: Be proud! Look about! What you see is the work of your own hearts and hands. You have carved a magnificent castle from rock, hewn a home from the hard earth. You have built a dream! We stand in awe at the immense stature of Nobby ingenuity, dedication, and service over these past ten seasons. Your selfless effort will benefit Nobbies for untold generations. Mere words could never express my deep admiration and gratitude for your sacrifice. Tonight, I make this solemn pledge: My life belongs to you, each breath drawn for you and yours. Thistledom is our land, our home, our love."

Queen Astrid moved quickly to her husband and together, waved to applause that threatened to topple the huge columns embracing them all.

As Bo rose, there was an immediate silence. Every eye focused on the dais. "Tonight is a special moment in time. Please go to the courtyard. The beam of the North Star is about to appear beginning another *Festival of Light*. It will be the first celebrated from our new home. I promise that tonight will be unforgettable!"

Cool night air was exhilarating under a clear black sky aglow with millions of twinkling stars. With the main gate closed, Nobbies spread out across the courtyard. Members of the Royal Guard stood watch on the walls. All eyes turned northward in anticipation of the beam's first glow. There was stunned silence when a glow directly above showered soft light down upon them, turning the granite courtyard into a dazzling arena bathed in pale blue light. Bo's reassuring voice calmed everyone:

"It's okay! Don't be afraid! For the first time, tonight you see the beam while standing in it! Yes, it's true! Spread out! Raise your eyes and arms toward the heavens. Feel its soothing warmth. Breathe deeply and let your limbs relax. Enjoy the moment! What better place to celebrate the *Festival of Light* than in the beam of the North Star. What better place for the Castle of Thistledom! Nobbies everywhere will know that the heart of Thistledom beats in the beam!"

## DuBois Castle—Homecoming

After an initial wave of disbelief, the thrill and wonder of discovery took over. Healing rays soothed tired bodies and lifted already high spirits to heavenly heights. The festive decorations hanging below in the Great Hall paled to the dazzling display of color now swirling in dance around the courtyard. Nobbies would celebrate until the beam faded with the dawn, but their joy would remain. Since this was a special cycle, the beam would return two more evenings. Irene retired to the balcony of her private chambers high above the celebration. Tears welled in a torrent of emotion. Below everything became a blur of beautiful color. She strained to capture everything. With a deep sigh, she wiped her eyes. Zygmunt would have been so proud.

Bo was always excited to see the beam, but even more so this time. The crypt room, just under the courtyard, had been filled with crystals and precisely positioned to absorb rays from the beam. He hoped that the energy of the beam could be captured and stored within the crystals as was sunlight. A trip to the crypt confirmed his dream. The pool of crystals glowed much brighter than earlier. He was ecstatic! With this store of renewable energy, he knew that the tiny crystals could be re-energized and used over and over to replace candles in the castle, and eventually, perhaps throughout the kingdom. He knew there would be other uses, as well, but they would come in another time. For now, he must help Theo solidify the kingdom and transfer this new knowledge to younger minds.

The *Shiver* season seemed shortened, due no doubt to the warmth generated by a kingdom still pulsating with pride and goodwill. *Awakening* was spectacular in the clear mountain air. Nature was not alone in its outpouringof new life. All of Thistledom shared a wonderful time of peace and unparalleled prosperity. The accomplishments achieved at DuBois Castle seemed to open endless possibilities.

A group of young Nobbies came to Bo for guidance on design ideas for subterranean housing. He met with them, encouraged them to move forward, and then established a Science Academy to encourage development of new ideas and building materials. Shortly, whole subterranean villages sprouted around the mountain top. It was amazing! There was a thriving economy all around a giant castle in a sprawling kingdom, and the activity was hardly noticeable. Nobbies lived in such close harmony with nature, their presence to the outside world was virtually invisible.

With such a concentration of Nobby families so close to the castle, Queen Astrid converted one of the lower level wings to classrooms. The children entered through the two hidden access tunnels on each side of the mountain. Irene worked with young Nobesses to establish a health clinic. They prepared and distributed health teas, spices, medicinal herbs, and poultices.

The Royal Guard also expanded its role, no longer just serving as border lookouts. They helped transport school children and worked on public safety projects. Younger members were assigned as pages in and around the castle, adding color, spirit, and efficiency to all

## DuBois Castle—Homecoming

activities. From all reports it appeared that the bogs had been abandoned by the Troggs. There had been no activity for several cycles. Nobbies traveled in complete safety once again. It was a wonderful time to live.

Prince Alec, now twenty-four, was very interested in science. Like his uncle Bo, he favored his grandmother Irene in temperament and size. He loved the castle and was an endless fount of ideas. Young Alec began to meet regularly with his father and uncle Bo to talk about the castle and to discuss some of his own ideas. Before long, they were drawing plans for two huge towers and a moat. Both would be large, lengthy projects. It became clear, however, that neither could even begin until another matter was settled. They had to survey the large underground lake and learn how to redirect the stream. It had to flow into one end of the moat and then return to the lake at the other. Working with such a large body of water was a new challenge. They knew little and needed to learn much more. They agreed to study the underground lake first beginning at its cave entrance on the western face of the mountain just above the spot where the stream flows from the mountain.

Three cycles have passed—a time of great growth and tranquility. But as we know, the rhythm of life seems to demand change. Unfortunately, change is not always for the better. Sometimes, it even hurts. It is the time of Harvest. The crops are bountiful and life is great. Castle DuBois is the center of a thriving kingdom.

After a day of welcoming new Nobbesses to a recently expanded health center, Irene returned to the main castle. She dined with the royal family, which now included Prince Alec's young wife, Deidre. With a smile, she retired early for the evening. It would be her final farewell. Queen Mother Irene died in her sleep. Her loss brought great sadness throughout the kingdom. She had helped so many through her knowledge and goodness. All admired the always gentle and kind Lady Irene with the beautiful voice, the wife of Zygmunt, mother of King Theodore and Bo, and grandmother of Prince Alec.

At first, Bo and Theodore planned to return their mother to her beloved Thistleville, the new center of the Province of Thistle. But instead, they followed a suggestion given by Prince Alec. He and members of the Royal Guard went to Thistleville and brought the remains of Zygmunt back to the castle. In a grand ceremony that first welcomed him to the castle amid trumpets and drum roll, Zygmunt and Irene were laid side by side in a specially prepared vault beneath the floor of the Throne Room. Together once again in a place of honor, they would serve as strong and constant reminders of the true meaning of Nobby life and love. Inseparable from Thistledom, Zygmunt and Irene would be remembered forever in the Kingdom of Thistledom as the sowers of "the seeds of the promise."

# Pillars Fall in Thistledom

It is during *Rain* in the following cycle that King Theodore decides to visit all the outposts of the Royal Guard. He is beginning to question the wisdom of remaining hidden and isolated. Perhaps Thistledom should attempt to reach out, discover, and develop alliances and relationships. Perhaps it is time to withdraw this surveillance net and reassign the young Nobbies to more exciting roles within the kingdom. A special troop of twenty castle guards accompany him and Bo along with James and John, Commanders of the Guard. They will travel by land using carriages strapped to the backs of large white-tailed deer. They plan to assess the facilities used by the Guard and survey conditions along the borders of the kingdom. Meetings with Vice Chancellors and Provincial Councils are scheduled, first in Faba, Ogle, and then in Kora, and finally Thistle. Chancellor Adrian travels ahead to prepare the way and to organize each event.

On the morning of the third day in *Flowers*, King Theodore, Bo, and a small entourage departed through the main gate. Prince Alec and Deidre stood at his mother's side as they waved goodbye. He was in charge until his father's return. This was an important trip. The weather was beautiful. The forest was bursting with new growth. Songbirds were everywhere. The large bucks moved slowly and gracefully along the castle roadway, then darted into the trees and directly down the eastern slope of the mountain. The nearly straight-line descent intersected Binder's Trail at the bottom. It had been a very long time. Not much had changed.

As they neared the spot where Binder lay, Bo, Theo, and their childhood friends, James and John, all glanced upward. The old tree was still standing taller than ever. The crusted nests were still there gently rocking in the breeze. So much had happened since those fateful days of their youth. Life had been so much simpler then. Now it was hard even to imagine life without Thistledom and DuBois Castle. Bo and Theodore stopped for a moment of silence in respect for the memory of Binder. They remained for several more as their thoughts moved to their mother and dad. The pain of separation somewhat over time, but the nagging ache never really goes away. Memories remain the tie that binds and for them, they were many and marvelous. With tears in their eyes and a tip of the hat, they were on their way.

The deer passed the edge of the bog without incident. Reports were accurate. The Troggs were gone. Bo and Theo could see the outline of Trogg Island still visible in the midst of many smaller islands that had since risen from the swamp floor. It was a great comfort to know the bog was uninhabited. It made everything in Thistledom better.

As the party moved steadily northward, they passed scores of sentinel perches cleverly hidden. James and John had trained these young Nobbies well. A visit from the king, himself, however, was something very special. King Theodore was deeply moved by their honest display of loyalty, commitment, and personal sacrifice. He gave each a gold chain holding a polished coal pendant. The figure of a great horned owl in flight with a snake clutched in its talons was etched on each one.

King Theodore and his party continued northward five more days stopping at dozens more Nobby posts along the way. Finally, they arrived in Copper Creek, the center of the Province of Faba, and home of Alec's beautiful young wife, Deidre. This was Theodore's first visit to Faba as king. He was embarrassed at all the attention. His most difficult task was to let others wait on him. It was not in his nature to sit back and watch others work. He was a Nobby of action. He held back, however, but it was not easy.

King Theodore met briefly with the Vice Chancellor and Provincial Council. The miners and smelters of Faba had contributed a great deal to Castle DuBois, especially the amazing fire-hardened clay ducts used in the heating system. Many beautiful handcrafted vases, pots, and dishes used throughout the castle had also been produced by local artisans. King Theodore thanked the Elders for their leadership and applauded local leaders and citizens for their selfless generosity. In turn, they presented him with a large picture of the Thistleville tavern made from hammered copper, beautifully framed in chestnut wood. King Theodore was speechless. The tavern had played such an important role. Bo rose to his feet and thanked the Elders again. He promised that the picture would hang in the Throne Room overlooking their parent's final resting place. It would be a most fitting tribute.

Before departing for Ogle, King Theodore also talked with Deidre's parents assuring them that she was well and a most welcome member to the royal family. He was also relieved to learn that there had been no incidents involving missing Nobbies or unusual events at the mines. All was well. They could stay but one day at Copper Creek. This was to be a long trip, and Chancellor Adrian awaited them in the town of Oglebryne, another three days' ride to the north. So, with regret, the royal party departed.

King Theodore had spent considerable time in Oglebryne many cycles earlier organizing a Regional Council and courting a certain young Nobbess named Astrid. He had many fond memories. They had been traveling ten days now, so it was good to know a day of meetings and ceremonial dedications would be followed by a full day and night of rest.

The salt miners of the Region of Ogle could take credit for most of the underground design and excavation of DuBois Castle. Their experience using a grid pattern alternating huge block columns of earth with large excavated caverns was invaluable. King Theodore thanked them for their very hard work. He was surprised and overwhelmed when the Nobbies of Ogle presented two wall-size tapestries bearing the likenesses of his father and mother, and he thanked everyone in Ogle for such a caring gift. These tapestries would hang on the great wall in the Throne Room. The visit to Ogle was very satisfying, and the brief rest did wonders. Amid a cheering throng, King Theodore and party departed Oglebryne in late morning. Chancellor Adrian decided to travel with them to Kora. It was a good feeling because they were now heading home.

The Province of Kora also was special; it was the birthplace of Lady Irene, Mother of the Royal Family DuBois, and many relatives still lived there. All were so proud of Theodore and Bo. The Nobbies of Kora were also miners who worked underground coal fields through a maze of tunnels and vertical shafts. This knowledge helped link together the many underground levels beneath the castle. They had built the stairways and slides. Kora was also the site of large crystal mines. Without this resource, Bo would not have developed the special protective coatings used on the castle roof. There also would be no lighting system in the castle. Most important, rockwood could never have been be cut.

Two days and nights were spent visiting a handful of villages and mining sites. King Theodore also stopped to thank two Nobby artists who had carved and engraved the owl pendants. At an evening dinner, the Vice Chancellor of Kora presented King Theodore with two gold rings set with crystals in the shape of the Royal Crest. As king and queen, the Nobbies of Kora wanted him and Astrid to wear them at all royal functions. They were exquisite. He was deeply moved.

The final leg of the journey took them back south near the castle, but along the far western border of Thistle Province. King Theodore released Commander James and half of the Royal Guard so they could take gifts and other excess travel supplies directly to the castle. It made no sense to carry them farther. With Bo and Chancellor Adrian, Theo and Commander John would continue. They would return to the castle the following evening. The parties split.

The lower region of Thistle Province had large tracts of forest including birch, maples, poplars, giant elms, and an endless variety of fruit trees. Like the eastern border, there were also vast marshy areas of swamp and bogs. Sentinels of the Royal Guard maintained posts here as well, but not quite as many as on the other side of the Kingdom that ran parallel to Trogg Island and the bog. King Theodore was relieved that the borders were secure. He met many Nobby sentinels and distributed more owl pendants. Their dedication and vigilance were gratifying. He knew the kingdom was safe.

They spent the night in the small village of Elmtwig catching local Nobbies by surprise. The sincere warmth and spontaneity of their hospitality and generosity, however, was not a surprise. It was probably the most relaxing evening of the entire journey. Sharing a potluck meal and stories at the tiny village hall brought back wonderful memories of similar evenings at the tavern in Thistleville. So much of Nobby history lay in their rich storehouse of country tales and folklore. They stayed up much later than planned. It was just too much fun, and besides, sometimes you just have to enjoy the present moment. Like childhood, it will never return. Late next morning, after inviting the entire village of Elmtwig to the castle as special guests for the next *Festival of Light*, King Theodore and Bo waved happily and disappeared into the woods.

    A bit tired from the night before, the small party rode quietly. Less than two hours later, however, an eerie calm filled the woods. Even birds were silent. The deer became anxious and skittish. The trail, which had been rising steadily as it moved northward toward Thistleville and the castle, dipped through an isolated wetland. It was not a swamp, but was filled with dense brush, tall weeds, and some standing water. There was an opening in the center of this small valley, like a large room where several trails crisscrossed.

    Without warning, the calm was shattered by an onslaught of club-wielding, screaming Troggs. They came from everywhere: underbrush, weeds, behind trees, and even limbs high above the trail. Large, snarling doogles ran at the Nobbies from the sides, jumping high in the air and hurling themselves headlong into the deer. Barking and howling, they bit the deer with gaping, powerful jaws. Nostrils flaring and eyes wide with fear, the panicked deer lurched and lunged in different directions. But as they tried to escape, other Troggs jumped up from the tall weeds in a second line of attack, sending the frenzied deer back to the center of the trail. Leaping doogles bombarded the deer, and their sharp spiked collars tore long gashes in the carriages strapped on their backs.

With clubs and doogles whirling all about, Commander John spotted an opening. It was their only chance. He directed his large buck toward it waving for the others to follow. He hurdled several fallen trees, as well as angry Troggs. Seeing the escape route, the other deer instinctively turned toward freedom. But before the mount carrying King Theodore and Bo could move, two large doogles slammed into its right side. The force knocked the big buck to its knees. Bo and Theodore flew headfirst onto the ground. Screaming and swinging their clubs, the Troggs charged. Bo stood quickly in front of Theodore and pointed his finger at them. Surprised at this sudden unexpected defiance, they stopped and fell back. Even the doogles retreated in fear. He grabbed the reins as the deer staggered to its feet and motioned for Theodore to climb aboard.

Theo rose from the ground. Stunned from the fall, his head had been cut, and blood trickled down his face. As he stumbled toward Bo, a young Trogg lashed out catching a clawed finger in the chain hung around his neck. King Theodore felt the pressure and in one powerful burst, swung free and jumped onto the deer. The chain broke and the pendant fell to the ground. There was no time to retrieve it. Veins throbbing with anger, Theo reached his

## Pillars Fall in Thistledom

strong arm down to grab Bo. But instead of grasping his hand, Bo turned the reins loose and slapped the deer on the side of the head. In a heartbeat, the buck bolted, ran over the young Trogg, and followed the others to safety. Helplessly glancing back over his shoulder, Theo's eyes met Bo's for but a moment. Bo was smiling. Then in a flurry of motion, Theo saw a club fly through the air and strike Bo in the back of the head.

The large buck, crazed with fear, raced headlong after the others. Barely hanging on, King Theodore tried to stop him and go back for Bo, but it was impossible. The buck raced wildly away. Shortly, King Theodore caught up with the others as they tended the deer and regrouped. It was not possible to go back for Bo. Commander John suggested they ride to Thistleville for help. Time was most important. King Theodore was already planning a counter attack to free Bo. The whole village was shaken and angered by the unprovoked attack and capture of Bo. Every Nobby wanted to join in the retaliation. King Theodore understood well their anger, anxiety, and frustration, but he knew outright retaliation was not possible.

He had only one objective. *Free Bo!* The best chance to do that was a silent and swift return to the site of the ambush by a small raiding party. There was no time to wait for help from the castle. So with his head wrapped, King Theodore and Commander John selected three members of the Guard and prepared to leave. He sent Chancellor Adrian back to the castle to alert Prince Alec and to help handle things until he returned. Nobby sentinels around the perimeter of the entire kingdom were placed on full alert.

The depth of King Theodore's anger was frightening. Entering the tavern, he went to the kitchen and without uttering a word, picked up the largest knife he could find and slid it through the belt looped around his waist. Fire shot from his eyes as he returned to the village square. It was getting late and would be a long night.

The forest was quiet. The deer fanned out and moved without a sound. It was nearly dark when they approached the site of the ambush. The foul smell of Troggs and doogles still lingered in the air. It took a lot of effort to hold the deer steady. King Theodore dismounted and carefully studied the spot on the trail where he had last seen Bo. There was blood on the ground, but was it his or Bo's? There was no way to tell. He remembered his pendant and stooped to examine the ground more closely. He looked all around. He saw nothing. It too was gone. Returning to his mount, King Theodore pulled a scarf out of his satchel and tied it to a tree. He'd be back!

Trogg footprints and doogle marks were all over. It was impossible to determine the direction they had taken Bo. King Theodore remembered the Trogg huts and realized there must be others in the swamps on this side of the mountain as well. So without delay, he mounted the deer and headed southwest to the swamps and bogs. He was very worried. There had been no communication from Bo. This was not like him. Something was very wrong.

## Pillars Fall in Thistledom

The forest was dark. Storm clouds blotted out the moon. It was a real test of Nobby vision. King Theodore didn't seem bothered. He moved steadily and confidently on a straight line to the southwest. When they finally rode into the clearing at the edge of the tree line, the swamp lay just below. He noted immediately a bad sign. No campfires! The Troggs were not there! Angry, frustrated, tired, and worried, he decided to split the search party into two groups. He took two members of the Guard and rode farther south. Commander John and the other Guard rode north. Campfires would be the key. Sound the alert as soon as they were spotted. Time was becoming an enemy.

The search parties rode all night. They found nothing. At dawn, they rejoined and decided to move directly east across the southernmost border of the province. They rode quickly now covering large amounts of ground. They found nothing. Not a single sign of the Troggs! Not a single word from Bo! Nobby sentinels had nothing to report either. It was a very disturbing situation. Where had the Troggs gone? Why no contact from Bo? They continued the search all afternoon and again into the night. Exhausted, they finally rested a few hours at daybreak. King Theodore had never felt so helpless and stymied in his life. But then, it was the first time in his life without Bo. Chancellor Adrian and Commander James organized search parties at the castle, and after convincing a very troubled Prince Alec to stay at the castle, they worked their way south to meet King Theodore. No luck! Everyone continued the search throughout all of *Suntime* to no avail. Bo was gone without a trace. Life in Thistledom was no longer the same. King Theodore suffered the most, frustrated by his inability to find and rescue Bo. He had tried everything. Nothing could comfort him. He was consumed by grief.

The *Color* Season had arrived. Soon, the *Shiver* season would follow. Prince Alec could not wait for the next *Suntime* quarter. Another full cycle of pain and grief was unthinkable. In a last desperate effort to find some answers, Prince Alec asked Grandfather Adrian to take him to the site of the attack. He invited select staff members from the Science Academy to join him. Perhaps another long careful look might uncover missed clues or some new bit of information. Deidre and his mother were upset with this decision, but knew that Alec would not be dissuaded. They knew in their hearts that he was right. Something had to be done. Alec was their only hope. On the morning of the tenth day of *Colors*, in the company of Commander John who also had witnessed the attack, and a contingent of Royal guards and scientists, the search party mounted two dozen deer and headed southwest. It was a long shot, but Alec was hopeful. One must never lose hope.

The land in the province of Ogle was as beautiful as ever, filled with late blooming flowers and the bright colors of early changing leaves. Apple and pear trees still held good ripe fruit. There were many species of birds and lots of squirrels, rabbits, and pond life. These were all positive signs that nature was in good balance. All animal life was active and noisy, so they sensed no dangers. Uncle Bo had taught Alec how to read these signs. It was a most painful thought. He surely did miss his uncle and all the good that surrounded him. Nothing had been the same since his disappearance. Alec knew in his heart that nothing could ever be the same for his father without the reappearance of Uncle Bo.

They rode quickly and undisturbed throughout the day. It was hard to keep focused on the coming task when surrounded by such natural beauty. The rest of the world went on with life while they struggled to escape from the past. Alec couldn't help think what Uncle Bo would do if his father had gone missing instead. Everyone always remarked how he was so like his uncle Bo. Why then couldn't he solve this horrible puzzle? What happened to Uncle Bo, and where was he now? Where were the Troggs? Physical beings do not just vanish into thin air. There must be answers out there! Even dead bodies must be somewhere.

They stopped at dusk to set up camp in a stand of blue spruce and pine trees. The foliage was so dense and fallen needles so thick, it felt like they were in a carpeted room. The deer roamed the adjacent pasture for the night. They had been trained well by Uncle Bo. After a very light evening meal, members of the guard set up watch details. The rest of the party tied hammocks in the trees and settled down for the night. The combination of cool night air and the intoxicating scent of pine soon overwhelmed the senses.

Alec peered into the stillness wondering what the morrow would bring. His thoughts rushed to Deidre and his mother to put their hearts and minds at ease. Then he returned to thoughts of Uncle Bo. The unknown is a terrible thing. It gnaws at your mind, saps your strength, and robs you of both the present and the future. It is difficult to combat because it has neither face nor flesh. The unknown is indefinable, the worst of all phantasms because it is at the same time both real and imaginary—a nagging invisible force that causes tremendous pain to mind, body, and spirit. Alec knew well that it could also maim and kill—truly a force to fear and avoid. What would he find tomorrow? Were there any answers out there? Was Uncle Bo alive somewhere? Alec laughed softly as he pulled his blanket over his head to cut off a cool north wind. *Troggs are not the only ones who can disappear without a trace. No one would ever know Nobbies are here tonight.*

Alec's body slept, but his mind would not succumb. Thoughts of his ailing father, the nagging unknowns surrounding Uncle Bo, concern about his mother's pain, the anxiety Deidre felt, and his own worry over unknowns awaiting them weighed heavy on his heart. He wished Uncle Bo had given him just half his powers. Inevitably, his thoughts also rambled back to happier days with grandparents, parties, and special moments in the light of the beam. How quickly life's fortunes can change. There is no defense against it. Since we cannot control fate, we can only manage it—good or bad. We do the best we can and then…we must move on.

The Royal Guard never slept. Trained Nobby eyes saw every movement as the deer grazed and night creatures moved about on the ground and in the air.

## Pillars Fall in Thistledom

A quarter moon and star fields helped. They knew the importance of this mission. It was not so much solving a mystery as safeguarding Prince Alec. It was clear to many that the future of the Kingdom was already in his hands. They trusted him, but even the Guard had its own nagging fear. Could they trust themselves to have the power to defend him against unknown forces? Vigilance, however, was their mantra and defense their strength. They had learned well. Mutual trust now bound them together to face whatever.

"Prince Alec. Wake up. Prince Alec."

Prince Alec, startled from his thoughts, turned quickly to jump from his hammock, but strong arms held him in place. A gloved hand covered his mouth.

"Shhh… Prince Alec, don't make a sound! A large group of Troggs is approaching our camp from the west. They are coming right at us!"

Prince Alec nodded and dropped to the ground. Quickly, the others were awakened in similar fashion. As they pulled hammocks to the ground, they quickly slid on their boots and jackets. Glancing quickly through the branches, Prince Alec knew immediately that their only chance was to remain invisible. He saw the deer on the far side of the pasture. They too had seen the Troggs. Without the deer, there was no escape. Uncle Bo once explained that neither Troggs nor doogles see well. For their sakes, he hoped Uncle Bo had been right.

Everyone fell to the ground next to tree trunks and hurriedly covered themselves with pine needles hiding both bodies and scent. Now the waiting game began. As the caravan approached, they saw doogles pulling carts loaded with cooking pots and bags. Younger Troggs rode, but all others walked. The strange jumping motion of the doogles caused the carts to jerk forward at each stride rattling both pots and wheels. The entire group was not well organized. Older youngsters and younger doogles were scattered all about as the band moved closer. At least two hundred were in the party. With so many walking on the fringes of the main column, Alec knew the chances of discovery were great. Coming straight from the west, undoubtedly the caravan would pass them on both sides. Even breathing became dangerous.

The lead Trogg groups were now directly in front of their tree camp—close enough to see their faces and features. They were huge creatures, four to five times larger than Nobbies—very hairy with pointed ears and round red eyes. The larger Troggs wore heavy boots. Youngsters had strapped sandals. Their clothing seemed tattered or very loose fitting. By their appearance, Troggs were not likely to be friendly.

Some of the doogles relieved themselves on the outer ring of trees. They were large ugly beasts with thick muscular necks and a terrible odor. Except for Commander John and his grandfather, none of them had ever seen a doogle. The two front legs were natural, but the one huge back leg was not. Several seemed ready to enter into the stand but were called back by angry Trogg grunts. It was a near miss. Suddenly, as if on cue, the entire moving band swerved right and headed south away from the trees. Every Nobby remained still, scarcely breathing. Prince Alec, however, quietly spit into his hands, rubbed them quickly into the dirt and then on his face. Climbing a tree, he watched intently the procession below. Was Uncle Bo with this group? His thoughts went out as strong as he could project, but he sensed nothing. Uncle Bo was not there.

It was a close call, but what did it mean? Where had the Troggs been and where were they going? Was there another group left behind? Was Uncle Bo with them? They broke camp, rounded up the deer, and without hesitation, Prince Alec pointed straight west. There was a new spirit and purpose after this harrowing experience that brought clearer meaning, understanding, and focus. Each one of them had known Bo, now they knew his captors. This was no longer a "fishing" trip, it was a mission.

The deer galloped through large pastures and woodlands all morning. Prince Alec stopped by a small brook at midday to rest and water them. No one wanted lunch, however. A sense of urgency energized every heart. As the terrain began to slope in the afternoon, Commander John cautioned everyone. Soon, they would be near the site of the attack. He also warned that farther west, they would find wetlands and swamps—the likely home of other Troggs. It was important to slow down. They must reduce the possibility for ambush. Their mission was to observe and investigate—not to be seen or captured.

By late afternoon, the terrain became very wooded. Commander John and Adrian took the lead. They had no map, but their hearts and sense of loss lead them through trails directly to the small wetland and the spot of the ambush. Adrian pointed to the scarf King Theodore had left earlier. Members of the guard quickly established a safety perimeter. Not much daylight remained. Scientists from the Academy quickly surveyed the entire area and created a grid pattern. Tomorrow morning, they would comb every kernel of land, shrubs, and trees. Certain of their security, the Royal Guard prepared a light meal and then set the watch detail for the night. It had been a very long and strenuous day. Rest would clear heads and sharpen their focus for the work beginning at first light. Again, Nobbies disappeared into the trees. When all were asleep, Prince Alec woke his good friend, Timothy, eldest son of Commander John.

"Tim, the ambush site will be examined tomorrow. The swamplands, however, may hold many more clues, and we can't take everyone there. Will you go with me now? There is no time to debate this with my grandfather and your father. We're on our own!"

"Agreed! You alert the guards. They'll listen to you. I'll get the deer. Be careful! My father is a light sleeper."

As still as shadows, both walked the deer a safe distance from earshot and headed straight to the bogs below. Prince Alec needed answers. Now was the time—

perhaps the only time. In his heart, he knew that time was running out for his father and Uncle Bo.

Once again, a quarter moon and star fields provided plenty of light for Nobby eyes as they rode through the darkness. They searched frantically for campfires or other signs of life. Nothing! As they approached the first wetlands, the brightness of the heavenly lights doubled, reflecting now off the still waters below. Prince Alec recalled stories of Trogg Island on the eastern slope and how the huts were out in the bog away from the shore. It was safe to assume that Trogg behavior did not change from one side of the mountain to the other. The deer were familiar with swamps and moved easily deeper into the bog. If there were island huts, he would find them. Brightness, however, was good and bad. They could see farther, but the combination of light and scrub trees formed many shadows confusing land and water. He noted one other problem—they could leave a trail in water.

Luck was kind tonight. The deer instinctively headed toward the smell of tall grass and reeds. A dark mass loomed on the horizon. It grew darker as they moved closer. Soon they could see trees and distinguish one from another. The deer moved faster as the water became shallow. Suddenly, they stopped, peering straight ahead. There was danger. Prince Alec and Timothy cupped their hands around their eyes, straining to see through the darkness. Nothing! Then Prince Alec looked to the right, and there, a stone's throw away, was a row of reed huts. He realized then that they were heading directly into the night breeze, and the deer picked up the scent of huts straight ahead, but out of sight. The smell of the Trogg camp spooked the deer. They would go no farther.

There were no campfires. No signs of life. They dismounted and waded through water and mud to land and the first hut. Carefully pulling aside a sackcloth covering, they entered for the first time the world of the Troggs. The air inside was dank and foul smelling—akin to a mixture of burnt leaves and dead fish. They split and quickly searched through the three tiny rooms. The main room had a small table and four chairs made from bundled reeds. Wooden boxes along one wall held a few clay dishes and pots. The other two rooms were bedrooms with reed mattresses and more wooden boxes. They held a few clothing items, strange looking worn out boots, and some long pointed sticks. It was difficult to breathe, so they headed back to the opening. The cool night air felt so good!

In no time, Prince Alec and Timothy had entered a dozen huts. They were all the same. Troggs lived simply and had little use for anything but the necessities of life. The Trogg camp however, was much larger than they first thought. There were several rows of huts each leading from a large open space like the spokes of a wheel. There was a huge fire pit in the center with many tables and benches. Without a doubt, it was the center of the Trogg village. They saw large reed baskets hanging on wooden tripods with fire pits beneath them. Timothy looked more carefully and found they were covered on the inside with a hard sticky substance. When he saw one with clothing in it, he realized they were used for cleaning. Prince Alec looked behind several huts, but found nothing but junk and few broken wagon wheels. From the droppings, he knew the doogles lived behind the huts. Before heading back to the deer, he decided to go the far side of the clearing to look at a strange mound. Strange because it stood alone, and there was nothing like anywhere else. Half way across the clearing, he realized what it was—a grave. A mound of earth with stones piled neatly around was a grave. He was sure of it. Why was it placed in such a prominent spot? Who was buried there? Could it be Uncle Bo?

"Prince Alec, it will be dawn soon. We must leave now to get back before everyone wakes."

"You're right, Tim, but who is buried here? I must know!"

"There is nothing we can do now. We must leave!"

"Okay! But I'll be back! I must know!"

Once they cleared the bog and wetlands, the ride back to camp was fast and furious. Explaining their actions tonight would be tough enough. It would be worse if they were not back before dawn. Both knew there were nervous sentinels waiting up for them.

Shortly after first light, Commander John made his rounds. He checked the sentry posts, looked at the deer herd, and made sure his cook had a breakfast fire ready. It would be a busy day. What would they find? He closed his eyes for a moment to relive the ambush. Everything happened so fast amid so much noise, it was hard to remember many details. He had lead everyone out of the ambush, so he didn't see what happened to King Theodore and Bo. Had his actions been a mistake? He knew well the torment in King Theodore's mind. He shared the same dreams.

"Good morning, Grandfather! Did you sleep well?"

"Yes, Alec. How about you?"

"About as well as expected. I am anxious to begin. You must show and tell us everything you remember. You are the key eyewitness. Would you give us a briefing right after breakfast? It would help the Academy staff prioritize the search pattern."

"I will do my best. It all happened so fast! I don't know how we all survived! …and Alec, I was not here when your father and uncle fell. My mount was one of the first to follow Commander John's buck to safety. I didn't see what happened to Bo. This is a horrible memory for me."

"I know, grandfather. No one could have done more. I am grateful you escaped. Just do your best! Uncle Bo made a choice that day. He knew what he was doing. I only wish I knew."

## Pillars Fall in Thistledom

Immediately after eating and with Commander John standing next to him, Chancellor Adrian spoke.

"The Troggs attacked us over there in the center of the clearing where the trails intersect. It was early afternoon. We had not stopped for lunch because we didn't leave Elmtwig until late that morning. We saw no one as we entered the woods. Everyone was tired from the night before, so we rode quietly. I remember how good we felt and how calm it was as we entered this area. The deer became a bit skittish, but we paid little attention. Without any warning, Troggs and doogles attacked from all sides. They were everywhere! I remember Commander John waving for us to follow him. I know that King Theodore and Bo were riding together at the time a bit behind me. I'm guessing that they were right in the center of the clearing when the ambush occurred. The entire incident lasted only a few seconds. With all the sudden movement, swinging clubs, and the loud screaming and barking, our deer panicked. As the doogles rushed at us, the deer jumped and bucked and kicked wildly at them. I remember letting go the reins and grabbing the saddle with both hands. I did see that King Theodore and Bo had trouble hanging on because they were together. We were trapped! When I saw Commander John wave, I moved toward him and the others followed. There was no time to look back. We all assumed that King Theodore and Bo were right behind us. We didn't know they had fallen and that Bo had been captured until King Theodore caught up with us."

"Thank you, Grandfather. Do you have any thoughts, Commander John?"

"No! I agree with all Adrian has said. You can see that there is not much room to maneuver in this clearing. It's a marvel we all escaped! I only hope we find something today to help us find Bo—dead or alive. We cannot return to King Theodore empty handed."

For the next several hours, scientists and guards crawled on their knees over every kernel of ground. Except for a few randomly broken branches, not a trace of the ambush remained. The blood King Theodore had seen on the ground had long vanished with the rains. Morale was low. Prince Alec looked at Timothy. Now was as good a time as any.

"Grandfather, Commander John, there is something you must know. Throughout last night, Timothy and I discovered the Trogg camp west of here and searched it."

"What? Alec, you must never put yourself at such risk! You and Timothy could have been killed! Your father would be furious!"

"Grandfather, my father is dying with grief kernel by kernel. Thistledom is in peril. It is my duty to do all that I can to protect and defend it, my family, and my friends! You know this is true. Timothy knows it. I'm grateful for his courage and bravery. I have no time to waste debating. Last night, we located the camp. It is not far and is deserted—at least for a time. Timothy and I searched many huts but found nothing. Just as we were leaving, I discovered a lone grave in the center of the camp, not very large and unmarked. I must learn who is buried there. Could it be Uncle Bo? The Trogg band we saw yesterday morning came from this camp. The day is young. We must go back! I must know."

Adrian looked at his grandson and nodded in agreement. He knew Alec would be a great king.

Nobbies in a Trogg village was a strange uneasy sight. With sentinels posted, Timothy and the remaining guards scoured the rows of huts in the camp. There were many more than he had seen. Prince Alec and the others carefully dug into the mound. He was right. It was a grave.

Digging with their hands and small shovels, it didn't take long to reach a reed basket buried about one and a half thistle stems deep. They removed all the dirt around the top. At this point, two of the older scientists stepped forward and carefully removed the lid. There was a body wrapped in sackcloth. It certainly was too large to be Uncle Bo. Prince Alec was relieved but motioned for them to look further. They removed the body and unwrapped it, realizing immediately it was that of a young fully dressed male Trogg. He had been dead for some time. Prince Alec wondered who he was and why he was buried in the center of the village. He approached to take a closer look. The youngster was dressed in a crudely fashioned waistcoat, cloth shirt, britches, and black boots. Moving the body, however, had loosened something in the waistcoat pocket. He reached in and felt something hard and pliable. He pulled it out and fell back in shock. It was the gold chain that had hung around his father's neck. How did he get it? What was it doing in the pocket of a dead Trogg? Grandfather Adrian recognized it as well. Prince Alec recalled his father's words about those last moments with Uncle Bo:

"Two large doogles slammed into the right side of our mount. The force knocked the big buck to its knees. We both fell to the ground. The Troggs charged at us screaming and swinging their clubs. Bo jumped in front of me pointing his finger at them. They stopped and retreated. Even the doogles were afraid of him. Bo grabbed the reins and helped the buck to its feet. He motioned for me to get on its back. I had cut my head when I fell, but I got up and moved toward Bo. As I approached, I remember a young Trogg grabbing the chain around my neck. It snapped when I jumped onto the deer, and my pendant fell to the ground. I reached down to grab Bo, but he turned the reins loose and slapped the deer on the side of the head. The buck bolting for freedom trampled over a young Trogg. I looked back and Bo was smiling. The last thing I saw was a club strike him in the back of the head."

Intuitively, Prince Alec saw the connection.

"Prince Alec, your father will be pleased you recovered his chain!"

"That's true, Timothy, but it's of little value without the pendant. I don't see it anywhere."

"What do you want us to do, Alec?"

"Grandfather, we must return this young Trogg to his resting place, just as we found him. This old chain would mean little to my father without Uncle Bo or the pendant. It meant everything to this young Trogg. What we have seen here today must remain within each of us. Agreed?"

With that, Prince Alec returned the chain to the waistcoat pocket. Guards laid the body in the basket and replaced the lid. In a few moments, the grave stood again as a lone mound in the clearing. The chain was safe forever. Uncle Bo surely had been there. Where was he now?

With the lack of any real news about Bo after Prince Alec returned, King Theodore became more deeply distressed over the loss of his brother. His waking hours were tormented with personal blame at his failure to save Bo. His dreams were haunted by the vision of Bo's smile, a vision destined to be his last. King Theodore would never see him again.

At a time when the kingdom should be growing and rejoicing in its achievements, the loss of his mother and brother was too much to bear. King Theodore grew more melancholy and withdrawn. Astrid worked hard to distract him with ceremonial events and dinners. Prince Alec pushed his father to begin work on the towers, which would soar thirty zygs high. They completed plans and cleared ground for construction of foundations, but King

Theodore took no delight in the progress. Despite their very best efforts, no one could rekindle the spark in his heart. It had gone out with the loss of Bo.

Two cycles later, on the fifth of *Fire* in the midst of the *Color* season, his great heart simply stopped beating. Shock waves of sorrow and disbelief rolled throughout the kingdom. King Theodore had been the central figure in their lives for so many cycles. He was not only a giant in physical size, but in the power and majesty he embodied. He was the only King Nobbies had ever known. All saw him as the founder of the Kingdom, the architect of government, and the builder of the great DuBois Castle. Nobbies felt safe, confident, and proud. No one in Nobby history had done more to change the face of Nobby culture and embolden Nobby spirit. The loss of Bo had been tragic; loss of King Theodore was unbearable. Nobbies could not envision life without him.

It would be difficult to overstate the devastating impact of King Theodore's death. Nobbies stopped working. Commerce came to a standstill. Many did not leave their homes. Depression and anxiety engulfed the Kingdom. Nobbies had never experienced anything like this before, nor had the royal family. The situation was very serious. Uncertainty and fear ruled in Thistledom.

Crown Prince Alec was well known and much loved by Nobbies throughout the land. He was trusted and admired for his intelligence and dedication. The critical nature of this situation had little to do with confidence in Prince Alec's ability to lead. It reflected the depth of love and trust Nobbies had developed for their beloved King Theodore. Life without him was unimaginable.

Prince Alec was devastated by the loss of his father. Without a father and an Uncle Bo, he stood very much alone for the first time in his life—a frightening feeling. However, his personal grief and fears had to be checked. The Kingdom was in peril. The first order of business was to restore a sense of security, confidence, and pride throughout the land. Fear of the unknown is a most dangerous enemy for it lives within. The first challenge would be to replace the many unknowns haunting Nobby dreams with an immediate plan of action. Nobbies needed to know a schedule of events, what they were expected to do, and how their actions would help strengthen the kingdom King Theodore loved so much. Nobbies would need a new vision, one that would pay tribute to their fallen king while placing the burden of his unfinished dreams on their shoulders.

There's a time for joy and a time for weeping—both are related for one cannot be understood without the other. Prince Alec set the next three days as the official period of mourning. King Theodore would lie in state in the grand ballroom so that Nobbies could pay their respects both day and night. The Royal Guard would help coordinate travel from the provinces. The last two years had taught Alec much about the nature of grief. It is an internal disease of the mind and body. If left alone to fester and grow, it is fatal. Such is true for individual as well as kingdoms. Grieving is a healthy release that can and will cure itself given sufficient time and proper place.

The next morning, Nobbies began the longest lineup in their history. They stood in silence ten abreast as they entered the castle to file past the coffin. Parents brought children so they would remember King Theodore. A dozen Royal Guard stood at attention. The line stretched out of sight and moved non-stop for the full three days. On the fourth morning, the great doors to the grand ballroom were closed. Those who were lucky enough to be in the room at the time became the representatives of Nobbies throughout the land at the funeral service of the King.

Commanders of the Royal Guard, James and John, escorted Queen Astrid to her throne which was placed next to King Theodore's throne now draped in black. Prince Alec and Deidre followed. When everyone was seated, Prince Alec rose, bowed to his mother, and then knelt at his father's feet. He would need the strength and wisdom of both his father and uncle Bo for the task at hand. Nobbies needed a new vision. Would his be clear enough to turn their hearts?

"Dearest Mother, Lord Adrian and Lady Penette, My Beloved Deidre, Provincial Chancellors, and fellow Nobbies:

"Today is most difficult, a time every son wishes would never come—the burial of his father. Nobbies believe in the importance of family. It is the bond that holds this kingdom together; it is the singular support which nurtures and protects each of us permitting us to grow and flourish. Many roles are played in the dynamic of family life, each important and essential. Over an entire lifetime, one is not greater than the others, only different in function and timing. Even so, the role of father enjoys a special position of honor. The love we have for parents who have bestowed the gift of life, itself, is great. Inescapably, however, the intensity of that love and admiration will define the depth of our grief on that day we must say goodbye. We share the burden and pain of tremendous sorrow today as we prepare to bury a very special father, husband, son, and king. Your presence here in this chamber and the steady beat of millions of footsteps throughout the kingdom over the past three days are mighty testaments to the love we all share for him.

"The legacy of my father is legendary already. His very presence had cast a warm and comforting glow over all of Thistledom for many cycles. It is the brilliance of that glow that now casts such a deep menacing shadow as he leaves us. Do you remember his words when he first announced his vision for DuBois Castle?

'We are at a pivotal point in our history. Serious challenges face us and must be addressed. Our very survival could be at stake! It is a time for us to join hearts and hands, bodies and spirits, friends and neighbors, to form a bond the likes of which has never been seen before.'

"My father inspired us to focus on a single vision larger than life itself. Today, we stand in awe and silence by his side in the center of that dream. My uncle Bo shared every night of that dream. They were brothers. Inseparable! They complemented each other so well, they became two bodies with one spirit. The tragic loss of Uncle Bo was equivalent to losing his own life. It was only a matter of time. To this day the whereabouts of Uncle Bo remains a painful, frustrating mystery.

"The lessons of history are important. From the time of my grandfather Zygmunt, my family has lived by the maxim inscribed on the pendant worn around his neck: '*A Seeds Power Lies in Its Promise.*' We believe this! My father wore this pendant every day of his reign as a reminder of the power and promise the future holds for those who nurture the seeds of opportunity sown all around us in any given moment. The reality of DuBois Castle is your proof! That sacred pendant was lost the day it was ripped from my father's neck during the Trogg ambush. But that doesn't matter now. We shall never forget! It is inscribed on our crest and forever enshrined in the heart of every Nobby in the Kingdom of Thistledom.

"This is a new day, another pivotal point in our history! Serious challenges face us. There are many unknowns looming on the horizon. Yes, our very survival could be at stake! It is time for us to join heavy hearts and wringing hands, bowed bodies and saddened spirits, frightened friends and nervous neighbors, to form a bond the likes of which has never been seen before—even during the building of Thistledom. Our vision must be the protection, perpetuation, and growth of the kingdom for our posterity. It has been given to us. We must give it to our children. Seeds again have been planted. Who will nurture them? Who will help keep the power in their promise? I submit as my first official act as Crown Prince, here at the side of my father, First Ruler of Thistledom, a new maxim: *'Seeds of Promise Must Bloom in Adversity.'* As intense love can lead to the depths of grief, so too can our sorrow lift us to soar on the wings of success.

"Yes, we must rise to the challenges of the future. Remember, however, that we are Nobbies! We are never alone. We are a family! I ask you to walk with me to the base of the huge eastern tower. Castle DuBois, once only his dream, will now stand forever as his legacy. When we complete it, the great tower will be the gravestone of King Theodore, first ruler of Thistledom. A Nobby whose dreams lifted a Kingdom to the heights."

As Prince Alec returned to his seat, his mother smiled. Deidre squeezed his hand, and the entire contingent of Royal Guards stood and saluted. Every Nobby in the room rose and turned in silent acclamation for their new king, Crown Prince Alec. He bowed his head in silent gratitude to his father and uncle Bo. His "new vision" was clear enough. Their hearts had turned.

An honor guard of eight lead by Lieutenant Timothy stepped forward, lifted King Theodore to their shoulders, and waited for the drum corps to takes its position at the front of the procession. Commanders of the Royal Guard, John and James, carried the Royal Crest of the Kingdom of Thistledom and the DuBois Family banner immediately in front of King Theodore. Prince Alec walked arm and arm between his mother and Deidre immediately behind his father. They were followed by Lord Adrian and Lady Penette, provincial chancellors, and Nobby representatives from across the kingdom. All walked to the slow deliberate rhythm of the drums. As King Theodore was placed in a special vault carved into the base of the tower, a fanfare of trumpets played a final farewell that rode the winds throughout the land. A grand and glorious era had ended; a new day was dawning. Prince Alec would stand alone at the forefront.

Two weeks later on the morning of the twenty-third of *Fire*, Prince Alec knelt in the Grand Gathering Hall. As he had long ago in a garden next to the tavern in Thistleville, Lord Adrian rose to speak:

"Fellow citizens, I am humbled to speak to you this morning. Many cycles ago, I stood before you to proclaim the coronation of King Theodore and my daughter, Queen Astrid—the first royal rulers of the Kingdom of Thistledom. Today, it is the privilege of a very proud grandfather to administer the solemn oath of office and to lay the mantle of regal authority across the strong shoulders of my grandson. Prince Alec, please rise and bow your head.

"By the will and consent of citizens throughout Thistledom, we name you head of the Royal Family DuBois and charge you with the power and responsibility of governing the sovereign Kingdom of Thistledom. It shall be your solemn duty to protect the realm, preserve the dignity of individual rights, and lead us forward to the future. In return for our solemn pledge of fidelity, and our promise to preserve, protect, and perpetuate the Monarchy of Thistledom and the rights of the Royal Family DuBois, do you, Alec DuBois, swear by He who created the heavens and earth, who set the beam of the North Star in place, and who guides all things with an inner rhythm and grace; do you swear to accept without reserve the regal rights, responsibilities, and role now offered to you and your descendants as our king?"

With tears in his eyes, Prince Alec spoke in a clear, strong voice, "In the name of my mother, Astrid, in memory of my father and uncle Bo, for the love of Deidre, and with eternal gratitude to you, grandfather, and for the glory of all the citizens of Thistledom: Yes! I do accept!"

Two young attendants holding a dazzling white cloth approached. Grandfather Adrian took it carefully and draping it over Prince Alec's right shoulder said, "Alec DuBois, receive this seamless mantle of finest lace as a symbol of the authority bestowed upon your person here today, and to your heirs in the tomorrows that will follow. And now, I ask that you and Deidre kneel before your thrones to receive the crowns of the Kingdom of Thistledom."

Queen Mother Astrid stood and slowly approached. Attendants presented two newly fashioned gold crowns laden with jewels. Her hands trembled as her father handed her the larger crown. She cradled it in her arms for a moment, then placed it upon her son's head. Her father then handed her the second, and she placed it softly on Deidre's bowed head. This was the moment!

This time, the Grand Gathering Hall erupted into cheers and dancing. There would be no holding back now! Thistledom had a new king and queen. The kingdom had endured a double blow but survived. A chorus of cheers rang out in succession. "Long live King Alec and Queen Deidre! Blessings to the DuBois family! Blessings to Nobbies everywhere! Thistledom forever!" Alec held Deidre's hand as they walked throughout the Grand Hall embracing everyone within reach. It was a great gesture of love and trust. This is how a family should celebrate. They were happy and Nobbies were ecstatic. After touring the Grand Hall and even adjacent corridors, King Alec and Queen Deidre walked back through the adoring crowd to their table on the dais. It was time for the banquet. The kitchens and bakeries had been working round the clock for days preparing a feast fit for a new king.

As the meal began, Deidre leaned over and whispered softly to Alec, "Enjoy the meal! By the way, I have a secret for you. This evening… *I'm eating for two*."

Grandfather Adrian left his post as Chancellor to become personal confidant and advisor to King Alec. He and Queen Mother Astrid became the family bond that would guide and support the young king helping hold the kingdom together through this uncertain period of transition and trial. The birth of Princess Kire on the seventeenth day of *Rain* the following cycle brought great joy to the royal family and Nobbies everywhere.

## Pillars Fall in Thistledom

"Lord Norbert," Emily sobbed. "What a great story! A baby in the castle! But it's also so sad. I can't believe we could lose a king and Nobby Master at nearly the same time. We're lucky the kingdom survived! I know that Prince Alec became king, but who became the Nobby Master?"

"It was a most difficult period in our history, that's for sure! Your question about the Nobby Master is a good one. The answer remains unknown to this very day."

With that, the room erupted in a flurry of questions:

"How can Nobbies get along without a Nobby Master?"
"Who finished building the two great towers?"
"Who built the moat? When was it finished?"
"How did King Alec control the streams?"
"Did the Nobbies follow the vision described by King Alec?"
"Did the Troggs ever return?"
"Did King Alec ever learn the identity of the young Trogg who was buried?"
"Was there any new information about Bo? Was he dead?"

"Children, these are all very important questions, but not possible to answer here tonight, unless we stay up all night!"

In a single chorus, they begged: "Please, Lord Norbert, tell us more! We can't wait! No one knows when will we all be together again! You must continue! Please, go on!"

"Children, as you are beginning to learn, there have been many players on our Nobby stage. Each was important. As you listen, note how each willingly became a stone on the pathway of Nobby history, so that others like us might follow in freedom and safety. It is our code of Nobby conduct - *service to others* - expressed in its purest and most powerful form. Listen and learn of love and lives shared, ...and prices paid. Understand the real source of power that is the Kingdom known as Thistledom, your home."

Queen Julia spoke for all: "We will listen well, Lord Norbert. Please tell us all you can, especially details about what happened with the Troggs and doogles?"

Lord Norbert nodded, but suddenly, as if he had seen a ghost, he peered into the shadows and warned:

"Thistledom has not always been the loving and peaceful kingdom you know today. Nobbies have paid dearly for this castle, our homes, and our security. It has been said that *A Seed's Power Lies in Its Promise*. This surely is true. Unfortunately, we have learned another truth as well from King Alec. The seeds of promise must also bloom in adversity—pruned by tragedy and nurtured by sacrifice if our Nobby world is to endure. Taking a very deep breath, Lord Norbert began an incredible saga about Thistledom now spanning six generations. As early chards of sunlight split the darkness, all began to understand the true meaning of King Alec's vision."

## Thistledom

### "Seeds of Promise Must Bloom in Adversity"

## Epilogue

King Alec had inherited a Kingdom in transition and trial. A devoted family, Queen Deidre, Queen Mother Astrid, and his maternal grandparents Adrian and Penette, stood at his side. He had lost a father and uncle to the Troggs, and he had sworn that he would make the kingdom safer by completing DuBois Castle's towers and moat and raising the level of security. The test for his forbearers had been to establish a kingdom, his was to be a more difficult one. He must maintain and perpetuate it—*without* a Nobby Master.

King Alec would be a "bridge" ruler between the past and the future. Undoubtedly, he was the best prepared king in the long storied history of Thistledom. His family roots and personal experiences went back to Zygmunt himself. His early life was molded by two historical giants: his father and uncle Bo. His maternal grandfather Adrian also had taught him much. He had been the administrative and logistical genius who had overseen the birth of the Kingdom and the construction of the castle and grounds. Now King Alec's task was to keep the dream alive.

Theodore and Bo had been the body and soul of Thistledom expanding Nobby life from villages and hamlets to four provinces, and then to a kingdom with a great castle and a royal family. Following a motto inscribed on a pendant given to their orphan father, "*A Seed's Power Lies in Its Promise*," they had lived fully in the present moment, but always with a vision for the future. King Alec's new vision did not diminish the truth or importance of this legacy. He challenged his generation and those that would follow to hold fast to the values of the past in a changing world. Adversity would become a troublesome neighbor, but if Nobbies were to endure, they must learn to live with it.

While standing alone admiring star fields on a clear dark night at the end of *Fire,* King Alec's thoughts raced wildly: *There are so many unresolved issues, will I ever find answers? Where are all the Trogg camps? Who was the young Trogg in that lone grave? Why did he have my father's chain? What happened to Uncle Bo? Is he alive or dead? Will I ever find him? Will Nobbies follow me? What can I do about the Troggs? Could we ever live together? How long will it take to finish the towers and moat? Am I ready to be a father? What will this child be? So many questions!* ...*If I am to lead Thistledom into the future, I must become the first seed to bloom in adversity.*

# Glossary

## Words, Terms, Tables, Charts & Map

## A

**acclamation,** n, A shout or salute of enthusiastic approval. An oral vote, especially an enthusiastic vote of approval taken without formal ballot: a motion passed by acclamation.

**accommodation,** n, The act of accommodating or the state of being accommodated; adjustment. Something that meets a need; a convenience. Room and board; lodgings.

**alleviate,** v, To make (pain, for example) more bearable.

**array,** n, An orderly, often imposing arrangement: an array of royal jewels.

**artisan,** n, A skilled manual worker; a craftsperson.

**avid,** adj, Having an ardent desire or unbounded craving; marked by keen interest and enthusiasm.

# Glossary

# B

**bedeck**, v, To adorn or ornament in a showy fashion.

**bequeath**, v, To leave or give (property) by will. To pass (something) on to another; hand down.

**bog**, n, An area having a wet, spongy, acidic substrate composed chiefly of moss and peat in which characteristic shrubs and herbs and sometimes trees usually grow. An area of soft, naturally waterlogged ground.

**breached**, v, To make a hole or gap in; break through.

**briar,** n, Any of several prickly plants, such as certain rosebushes or the greenbrier.

**buoyed**, v, To maintain at a high level; support.

# C

**chancellor**, n, Any of various officials of high rank, especially a secretary to a monarch.

**compress**, n, Medicine. A soft pad of gauze or other material applied with pressure to a part of the body to control hemorrhage or to supply heat, cold, moisture, or medication to alleviate pain or reduce infection.

**confidant**, n, One to whom secrets or private matters are disclosed.

**console,** v, To allay the sorrow or grief.

**councilor**, n, A member of a council, as one convened to advise a governor or king.

**craze,** v, To cause to become scared or excessively frightened.

**crude**, adj, Being in an unrefined or natural state; raw. Lacking tact or refinement.

**crypt**, n, An underground vault or chamber that is used as a burial place.

**cue**, n, A signal, such as a word or an action, used to prompt another. A hint or suggestion.

**custodian**, n, One that has charge of something; a caretaker: the custodian of a minor child's estate or property.

# D

**Dais**, n, A raised platform above the floor of a large room to give prominence to those seated on it.

**dank**, adj, Disagreeably damp or humid.

**deference**, n, Submission or yielding to the opinion, wishes, or judgment of another. Courteous respect.

**deft**, adj, deftly, adverb, Quick and skillful.

**deject**, v, To lower the spirits of; dishearten.

**disdain**, n, A feeling or show of contempt and aloofness; scorn.

**din**, n, A jumble of loud, usually discordant sounds.

**disclose**, v, To expose to view; uncover. 2. To make known.

**divulge**, v, To make known (something private or secret), reveal.

**douse** also dowse, v, To plunge into liquid; immerse.

**drone**, v, To make a continuous low dull humming sound.

**dub**, v, To give a name to facetiously or playfully; nickname.

**dwindle**, v, To become gradually less until little remains.

# E

**ebb**, v, To fall back from the flood stage. Decline or recede.

**ecstatic**, adj, Marked by or expressing ecstasy. Being in a state of ecstasy; enraptured.

**eerie** or eery, adj, Inspiring inexplicable fear, dread, or uneasiness; strange and frightening.

**elaborate**, adj, Planned or executed with painstaking attention to numerous parts or details.

**eloquent**, adj, eloquently, adverb, Characterized by persuasive, powerful discourse.

**elude**, v, To evade or escape from, as by daring, cleverness, or skill.

# Glossary

**embed**, v, To fix firmly in a surrounding mass.

**emblazon**, v, To adorn (a surface) richly with prominent markings: To make resplendent with brilliant colors.

**embody**, v, To give a bodily form to; incarnate. To make part of a system or whole.

**engender**, v, To bring into existence; give rise to.

**engulf**, v, To swallow up or overwhelm.

**ensemble**, n, A coordinated outfit or costume. A group of entertainers who perform together.

**entourage**, n, A group of attendants or associates; a retinue.

**eon**, n, An indefinitely long period of time; an age.

**epic**, adj, Surpassing the usual or ordinary, particularly in scope or size: Heroic and impressive in quality.

# F

**falter**, v, To speak hesitatingly; stammer.

**fanfare**, n, Music. A loud flourish of brass instruments, especially trumpets. A spectacular public display.

**festoon**, v, To decorate. Noun, a string or garland, as of leaves or flowers, suspended in a loop or curve.

**fibre** or fiber, n, A slender, elongated, threadlike object or structure.

**fidelity**, n, Faithfulness to obligations, duties, or observances.

**finery**, n, Elaborate adornment, especially fine clothing and accessories.

**fitful**, adj, Occurring in or characterized by intermittent bursts, as of activity; irregular.

**flail**, v, To wave or swing vigorously.

**flank**, v, To put (something) on each side of.

**fledgling**, adj, New and untried or inexperienced: a fledgling.

# Glossary

**foe**, n, A personal enemy. An enemy in war. An adversary; an opponent.

**foliage**, n, Plant leaves, especially tree leaves, considered as a group. A cluster of leaves.

**folklore**, n, The traditional beliefs, myths, tales, and practices of a people, transmitted orally.

**formidable**, adj, Arousing fear, dread, or alarm: Difficult to undertake, surmount, or defeat.

**fortnight**, n, a period of 14 days: two weeks.

**foul**, adj, Offensive to the senses; revolting. Having an offensive odor; smelly.

**fuse**, v, To mix together by or as if by melting; blend.


# G

**gamut**, n, A complete range or extent:

**garner**, v, To gather and store in or as if in a granary. To amass; acquire.

**gingerly**, adv, With great care or delicacy; cautiously.

**glean**, v, To collect bit by bit.

**gouge**, v, To cut or scoop out with or as if with a gouge.

**gourd**, n, Any of several trailing or climbing plants related to the pumpkin, squash, and cucumber and bearing fruits with a hard rind. The dried and hollowed-out shell of one of these fruits, often used as a drinking utensil.

**grandeur**, n, The quality or condition of being grand; magnificence: Nobility or greatness of character.

**gratify**, v, To please or satisfy.

**guise**, n, Outward appearance or aspect; semblance. Mode of dress; garb.

# H

**hallmark**, n, A mark indicating quality or excellence. A conspicuous feature or characteristic:

**harrowing**, adj, Inflicted with great distress or torment.

**havoc**, n, Widespread destruction; devastation. Disorder or chaos.

**headlong**, adv, head first: In an impetuous manner; rashly. At breakneck speed or with uncontrolled force.

**hearth**, n, The floor of a fireplace, usually extending into a room and paved with brick, flagstone, or cement.

**horde**, n, A large group or crowd.

**hysteria**, n, Excessive or uncontrollable emotion, such as fear or panic.

I

**illumine**, v, To give light to; illuminate.

**implement**, v, To put into practical effect; carry out.

**in residence**, The phrase means to live at one's home while performing a service. An artist "in residence."

**incessant**, adj, Continuing without interruption.

**incident**, n, A definite and separate occurrence; an event.

**incoherent**, adj, Lacking cohesion, connection, or harmony; Unable to think or express one's thoughts in a clear or orderly manner: incoherently ,adverb.

**inexhaustible**, adj, That cannot be entirely consumed or used up: Never wearying; tireless.

**infectious**, adj, Capable of causing infection. Caused by or capable of being transmitted by infection.

**ingenuity**, n, Inventive skill or imagination; cleverness. Imaginative and clever design or construction.

**inscription**, n, Something, such as the wording on a coin, medal, monument, or seal, that is inscribed.

**instill**, instilled, instilling, instills: v, To introduce by gradual, persistent efforts; implant.

**intuitive**, adj, Of, relating to, or arising from intuition. Known or perceived through intuition. Instinctive.

**inundate**, v, To cover with water, especially floodwaters. To overwhelm as if with a flood; swamp.

## J

**jostle**, v, To come in rough contact while moving; push and shove: To make one's way by pushing or elbowing.

## K

**kernel**, n, a Nobby linear measure (k) equaling one corn kernel; .25 inch; 0.64 centimeter.

**kernel bag**, n, a Nobby measure of weight (kbg) equaling sixteen ounces or one pound; 0.453 kilograms.

## L

**lade**, v, To load with or as if with cargo. To burden or oppress; weigh down.

**legacy**, n, Something handed down from an ancestor or a predecessor or from the past.

**lift**, n, A machine or device designed to pick up, raise, or carry something.

**lilt**, v,  To speak, sing, or play with liveliness or rhythm.  To move with lightness and buoyancy.

**lope**, v, To run or ride with a steady, easy gait.

**lurch**, v, To stagger.  To roll or pitch suddenly or erratically.

**lyrical**, adj, Expressing deep personal emotion or observations:  Highly enthusiastic; rhapsodic.

# M

**magnitude**, n, Greatness of rank or position: Greatness in size or extent: Greatness in significance or influence.

**maim**, v, To disable or disfigure, usually by depriving of the use of a limb or other part of the body.

**mainstays**, n: a chief support.

**makeshift**, adj:  a usually crude and temporary expedient : substitute synonyms see resource.

**malice**, n: desire to cause pain, injury, or distress to another.

# Glossary

**manifest**, adj, readily perceived by the senses and especially by the sight. easily understood by the mind.

**mantle**, n, a mantle regarded as a symbol of preeminence or authority.

**mastered**, v, to become master of : overcome.

**maxim**, n, a general truth, fundamental principle, or rule of conduct.

**medallion**, n, a large medal, something resembling a large medal.

**medicinal**, adj, tending or used to cure disease or relieve pain.

**melancholy**, n, an abnormal state characterized by irascibility or depression: depression of spirits.

**menacing**, v, to make a show of intention to harm; to represent or pose a threat to : endanger.

**militia**, n, a body of citizens organized for military service.

**minute**, adj, very small: infinitesimal.

**moat**, n, a deep and wide trench around the rampart of a fortified place that is usually filled with water.

**monumental**, adj, massive; also highly significant : outstanding: very great.

**mortally**, adv, in a deadly or fatal manner: mortally wounded.

**mused**, v, to become absorbed in thought.

# N

**new moon**, n, The moon's phase when it is in conjunction with the sun so that its dark side is toward the earth.

**Nobby**, n, Used in Thistledom as the name of very intelligent and resourceful little people who live in very close harmony with nature.

**noesis**, n, Each Nobby receives the power of noesis (the ability to communicate by thought) on his/her sixteenth birthday.

**noetic**, adj, describes the condition by which nobbies communicated solely by thought.

# O

**oath**, n, a solemn usually formal calling upon God or a god to witness to the truth of what one says or to witness that one sincerely intends to do what one says.

**oblivious**, v, lacking remembrance, memory, or mindful attention.

**omen**, n, : an occurrence or phenomenon believed to portend a future event : augury.

**ominous**, adj, : being or exhibiting an omen : portentous; especially : foreboding or foreshadowing evil.

**onslaught**, n, an especially fierce attack; also : something resembling such an attack.

P

**pandemonium**, n, a wild uproar : tumult pandemonium.

**paramount**, adj, : superior to all others : supreme; synonyms see dominant.

**parchment**, n, a parchment manuscript; in Thistledom, a translucent paper made from the bark of the Birch tree.

**peered**, v, to look narrowly or curiously; especially: to look searchingly at something difficult to discern.

**pendant**, n, 1 : something suspended: as a : an ornament (as on a necklace) allowed to hang free.

**penetrated**, v, to pass into or through: to enter by overcoming resistance: to see into or through b : to discover the inner contents or meaning of; to pierce something with the eye or mind.

**perpetual**, adj, continuing forever : everlasting.

**perpetuate**, v, : to make perpetual or cause to last indefinitely.

**pivotal**, adj, vitally important : crucial.

**plenary**, adj, fully attended by all entitled to be present.

**pliable**, adj, supple enough to bend freely or repeatedly without breaking.

**pneumonia**, n, : a disease of the lungs characterized by inflammation, malaise, cough, and often fever.

**portal**, n, door, entrance; especially : a grand or imposing one.

**posed**, v, to present for attention or consideration.

**poultice**, n, : a soft usually heated and sometimes medicated mass spread on cloth and applied to sores or other lesions; : to apply a poultice to.

**precaution**, n, care taken in advance: a measure taken beforehand to prevent harm or secure good : safeguard.

**precipitously**, adv, very steep, perpendicular, or overhanging in rise or fall: dangerously steep.

**predominant**, adj, having superior strength, influence, or authority.

**profound**, adj, having intellectual depth and insight: difficult to fathom or understand.

**prominent**, adj, readily noticeable : conspicuous: widely and popularly known: noticeable.

**prong**, n, a slender pointed or projecting part.

**properties**, n, a quality or trait belonging and especially peculiar to an individual or thing: an attribute common to all members of a class.

**providence**, n, divine guidance or care: God conceived as the power sustaining and guiding human destiny.

## Q

**quipped**, v, to make quips : gibe; to jest or gibe at.

## R

**rampaging**, adj, : to rush wildly about.

**ravine**, n, : a small narrow steep-sided valley that is larger than a gully and smaller than a canyon.

**recede**, v, to move back or away: to grow less or smaller : diminish, decrease.

**recounted**, v, to relate in detail : narrate.

**reeking**, v, to give off or become permeated with a strong or offensive odor.

**regal**, adj, of, relating to, or suitable for a king.

**rekindle**, v, to start (a fire) burning again.

**relentlessly**, adv, showing or promising no abatement of severity, intensity, strength, or pace : unrelenting pressure.

# Glossary

**reminiscent**, n, tending to remind : suggestive of some past event.

**renegade**, adj, individual who rejects lawful or conventional behavior;: unconventional.

**resin**, n, any of various solid or semisolid organic substances that are usually transparent formed especially in plant secretions and are used chiefly in varnishes, printing inks, and sizes and in medicine.

**resonant**, adj, continuing to sound: echoing.

**resplendent**, adj, shining brilliantly: characterized by a glowing splendor.

**rigors**, n, harsh inflexibility in opinion, temper, or judgment: the quality of being unyielding or inflexible : strictness (3) : severity of life : austerity b : an act or instance of strictness, severity, or cruelty.

**rogue**, adj, an animal being vicious and destructive.

# S

**safeguard**, v, to make safe : protect.

**sage**, n, one distinguished for wisdom.

**sanctuary**, n, a consecrated place: a place of refuge and protection.

**savor**, v, to taste or smell with pleasure : relish c : to delight in : enjoy.

**scaled**, v, to attack with or take by means of scaling ladders.

**scant**, adj, excessively frugal: barely or scarcely sufficient.

**scavenging**, v, to salvage from discarded or refuse material.

**scored**, v, to mark with lines, grooves, scratches, or notches.

**scrutiny**, n, a searching study, inquiry, or inspection: a searching look: close watch : surveillance.

**seer**, n, a person credited with extra-ordinary moral and spiritual insight.

**sentiment**, n, an attitude, thought, or judgment prompted by feeling.

**sentinels**, n, sentry: guard, watch; especially : a soldier standing guard at a point of passage (as a gate).

# Glossary

**shied**, v, to start suddenly aside through fright or alarm.

**shoring**, v, to give support to : brace — usually used with up.

**singular**, adj, distinguished by superiority.

**skiddish**, adj, A colloquial term to describe someone frightened, and therefore stumbling about as a result.

**smelters**, n, a worker who smelts ore.

**smolder**, v, 1 a : to burn sluggishly, without flame.

**solace**, n, to give solace: to console.

**solitary**, adj, being, living, or going alone or without companions: alone.

**somber**, adj, so shaded as to be dark and gloomy; conveying gloomy suggestions or ideas.

**specter**, n. a visible disembodied spirit : ghost: something that haunts or perturbs the mind.

**spooked**, v, haunt; to make frightened or frantic: scare; especially : to startle into violent activity (as stampeding).

**sprawling**, v, to lie thrashing or tossing about.

**stalling**, v, to put into or keep in a stall; to bring to a standstill: block.

**stark**, adj, barren, desolate: having few or no ornaments.

**stealth**, n, the act or action of proceeding furtively, secretly, or imperceptibly.

**stifling**, adj, suffocate: smother: to become suffocated by or as if by lack of oxygen : smother.

**strenuous**, adj, vigorously active: marked by or calling for energy or stamina.

**studded**, adj, to adorn, cover, or protect with studs; a boss, rivet, or nail with a large head used (as on a shield or belt) for ornament or protection.

**stymied**, v, to present an obstacle to : stand in the way of.

**sublime**, adj, lofty, grand, or exalted in thought, expression, or manner: of outstanding spiritual, intellectual, or moral worth: tending to inspire awe usually because of elevated quality (as of beauty, nobility, or grandeur) or transcendent excellence.

## Glossary

**surpass**, v, to become better, greater, or stronger than: to go beyond.

**swarm**, v, a great number of insects like honeybees emigrating together from a hive in company with a queen to start a new colony elsewhere or to attack a prey in defense of the hive or nest.

**synergy**, n, combined action or operation; condition such that the total effect is greater than the sum of the individual effects.

## T

**talons**, n, the claw of an animal and especially of a bird of prey.

**tapestry**, n, a heavy hand woven reversible textile used for hangings, curtains, and upholstery and characterized by complicated pictorial designs.

**thicket**, n, a dense growth of shrubbery or small trees: tangle.

**thistlebag**, n, a Nobby standard measure of weight equaling five bags of corn kernels (kbg); five pounds; or 2.27 kilograms.

**thistleleaf**, n, a Nobby standard of linear measurement equaling eight corn kernels (k); two inches; or 5.8 centimeters.

**thistles**, n, any of various prickly composite plants (especially genera Carduus, Cirsium, and Onopordum) with often showy heads of mostly tubular flowers.

**thriving**, adj, characterized by success or prosperity: to grow vigorously: flourish; to gain in wealth or possessions.

**tinged**, v, to color with a slight shade or stain : to affect or modify with a slight odor or taste

**tomes**, n, a volume forming part of a larger work; book; especially : a large or scholarly book.

**torrent**, n, a tumultuous outpouring : rush; a channel of a mountain stream.

**trace**, n, a mark or line left by something that has passed; a sign or evidence of some past thing.

**tracts**, n, an area either large or small: an indefinite stretch of land.

**tranquility**, n, free from agitation of mind or spirit.

**transcends**, v, to rise above or extend notably beyond ordinary limits; synonyms see exceed.

Glossary

**tripod**, n, a vessel (as a cauldron) resting on three legs; a stool, table, or altar with three legs.

**troll**, n, a dwarf inhabiting caves, hills, or swamp lands and bogs.

**turbulent**, adj, causing unrest, violence, or disturbance.

# U

**unanimously**, adv, being of one mind : agreeing; having the agreement and consent of all.

**uninhabited**, adj, unoccupied as a place of settled residence or habitat; no one lives in this locale.

**unparalleled**, adj, : having no parallel; especially : having no equal or match : unique in kind or quality.

**unprecedented**, adj, : having no precedent : novel, unexampled.

**unprovoked**, adj, incitement; an action that is not provoked, aroused, or stimulated.

**untimely**, adj, occurring or done before the due, natural, or proper time: too early : premature.

# V

**vast**, adj, very great in size, amount, degree, intensity, or especially in extent or range; synonyms see enormous.

**ventured**, v, to expose to hazard : risk, gamble: to proceed especially in the face of danger.

**vial**, n, a small closed or closable vessel especially for liquids.

**vigil**, n, a watch formerly kept on the night before a religious feast with prayer or other devotions: the day before a religious feast observed as a day of spiritual preparation: n act or period of watching or surveillance : watch.

**vigilance**, n, the quality or state of being vigilant.

**vigor**, n, active bodily or mental strength or force; intensity of action or effect : force.

**virtue**, n, conformity to a standard of right: morality: a particular moral excellence; a beneficial quality or power of a thing; manly strength or courage: valor; a commendable quality or trait : merit.

Glossary

**visionary**, adj, seer; : having or marked by foresight and imagination.

# W

**waned**, v, to decrease in size, extent, or degree: dwindle: to diminish in phase or intensity — used chiefly of the moon: to become less brilliant or powerful: dim.

**wavering**, v, to vacillate irresolutely between choices : fluctuate in opinion, allegiance, or direction.

**wee**, adj, very small : diminutive.

**winches**, n, any of various machines or instruments for hauling or pulling; especially a powerful machine with one or more drums on which to coil a rope, cable, or chain for hauling or hoisting.

**writhed**, v, to twist into coils or folds: to twist from or as if from pain or struggling; 3 : to suffer keenly.

John LaCroix

# Table of Nobby Measurement

**Linear Measure**

1 kernel (corn) (k) = .25 inch = 0.63 centimeter
8 kernels (k) = 1 thistle leaf (leaf, lf) = 2 inches = 5.04 centimeters
8 lfs = 1 thistle stem (ts) = 16 inches = 40.32 centimeters; 4.032 decimeters
3 ts = 1 Zygmunt (zyg) = 48 inches = 4 ft = 121.92 centimeters; 12.192 decimeters; 1.219 meters
132 zygs = 1 super zyg (Szyg) = 528 ft = 1/10 mile = 160.90 meters
330 zygs = 2½ Szygs = 1320 ft = ¼ chester (chtr) = ¼ mile = 402.33 meters
660 zygs = 5 Szygs = 2640 ft = ½ chtr = ½ mile = 804.67 meters
1320 zygs = 10 Szygs = 5280 ft = 1 chtr = 1 mile = 1609.34 meters = 1.61 kilometer

**Weight**

1 bag of kernels (corn) (kbg) = 16 ounces = 1 pound (lb) = 0.453 kilograms
1 thistlebag = 5 kbg; five pounds; 2.265 kilograms

**Notes of interest:**

Queen Julia is 4 lfs 6k tall = 9.5 inches tall = 24.13 centimeters or 2.413 decimeters.
Can you figure out the height of the perimeter walls, castle walls, chimneys, and towers?
How much does Zygmunt weigh? How tall are Troggs and what do they weigh?

**Average weights**:
Nobbies weigh about 2 kbg for each lf of height.
Troggs weigh about 3 kbg for each lf of height.
Doogles weigh about 3.5 kbg for each lf of height.
How tall are you and what would you weigh according to this standard of Nobby Measurement?

# Nobby Geographical Locations in Thistledom

The **Province of Thistle** is in the center of the Kingdom. It is the central province. The site of the castle is in a mountain that is about 5 chesters (miles) north of the village of Thistleville where the entire story begins. It is a region with vast tracts of forests. As the Kingdom is born Thistleville remains, but only as a small village from which the province now derives its name. The village of Elmtwig, hometown of Mickey Zimm is located here.

The **Province of Faba** is the region to the far north which is copper and iron country. Its main town is called Copper Creek and besides mining, it is known for pottery.

The **Province of Kora** is the region toward the west, the location of rich coal mines.

The **Province of Ogle** is the region stretching across the southern border and the location of salt mines. One of its famous towns is Oglebryne.

Immediately at the base of the mountain toward the east is the location of the huge eastern Bog. Nobbies travel down Binder's Trail to reach the Bog.

To the far west at the far edge of Kora is another swamp area called the western Bog.

John LaCroix

# Map of the Kingdom

John LaCroix

John LaCroix

The Kingdom of Thistledom is just beginning. The Family of Zygmunt and Irene DuBois is established as the Royal Family and their sons, Bo and Theodore, build the kingdom.

Princess Kire will become the first child of royalty born in Thistledom. Her birth under serious circumstances signals the beginning of a new era. Her life and contributions that will eventually change the course of Nobby history are chronicled in Volume II, "Seeds of Promise Must Bloom in Adversity."

John LaCroix

Princess Kire

John LaCroix

John LaCroix

John LaCroix